AF486012

JAMES SPINNER & THE PINNACLE MYSTERY

by

M. G. Princeily

Chapter One: The Stone Wall

Mr. and Mrs. Walsh living in a private land in a cozy two story family cottage house surrounded by beautiful

trees, mountains, and a sparkling river, which is a little far from the busy town, and the most normal

American Irish family to come across in the neighborhood. A community of nature lovers embracing the

breeze, nature, and the fishing for passion as they say. Their daughter excitedly runs into the kitchen asking

her mother which dress to wear for her fairy–themed birthday party in the evening. Ciara who just turned six

is very much of a princess herself, and her dream is to be a pageant queen when she grows up. Across the

kitchen, Mrs. Walsh said "I think the purple would do with the cake and balloon colors Ciara!"

The excited little voice responded "I thought so too mother!" She ran back up the stairs holding the two

dresses on each hand. Mr. Walsh walked into the kitchen grabbing a purpled icing sugar cookie on top of the

pantry worktop and asked Mrs. Walsh doubtfully "Have you seen James by any chance, my dear?"

"No I haven't seen him all afternoon!" she replied pilling up some rich fine dining ceramic plates from the

top cupboard giving quick eye contact as she was busy with arranging for her daughter's birthday party in a

few hours.

Mr. Walsh walked up the stairs and banged on an old pinewood door with a strong presiding voice saying

"James! James! Are you in there? Play it low and no magic with the plants and trees—do you hear me,

James?

 I want you to be normal and do not have any other surprises apart from giving a nice surprised birthday gift

to your sister!"

James seated on the bed inside the room putting down the book he was reading, took a deep breath, and

responded with a disappointed voice

"Okay!"

It was just an ordinary day for James, except it was the day he planned to change things to go in search of

wanting to have a normal life to how he thinks it's normal. The boy named James Spinner who will turn

fourteen in just two months has a healthy dark hair always neatly combed, and brown eyes. He is a friendly and peaceful-looking character but with a strong personality of confidence and strength that one could never think based on the first impression. He had a secret with a unique talent and capabilities, and calling it just a talent is just an understatement!

April 27th of 2008 (two days ago)

James was studying chemistry getting ready for his mock exam sitting on the roof in the time close to dusk. He could hear Mr. Walsh speaking about something to his wife which was a bit of a distraction for James. He was feeling cold with the breeze getting cooler and he closed the book wanting to get back inside and walked along the roof. He stepped into the ladder climbing down, and into his room through the window right next to the ladder. He kept the book on the table, shut the window, and went to bed tucking himself under the quilt for some shut-eye. As he closed his eyes and settled to sleep, he heard something tapping on the glass window. He got out of bed and walked up to the window and saw a red bird looking at him through the window flying outside right behind the glass. He opened the window wondering what it wants and saw a piece of paper tied on its leg with a piece of climber plant. . The most awkward it is to James as it may sound like a messenger from an old fairytale, he opened the window and untied the letter on its leg, and watched it fly away into the woods.

It's been two days and he still cannot imagine if he was dreaming of receiving a letter through a bird like the old tales. He slightly turned and glanced at the photograph of his mother kept on a wooden stool next to the bed. He put his hand underneath his pillow and took a folded letter, and opened the letter carefully. The handwritten letter is written so fine with crafted-like letters, and the large fonts at the bottom of the short letter with the most beautiful flow handwriting that says "Find your purpose at the secret Pinnacle and do what you feel is right!"

He folded and put the letter back under his pillow as he recalled the tragic night of him waking up years younger and walking into her mother's bedroom towards the bed surrounded by two maids wearing the traditional black and white maid uniforms who were looking at James while they weep, and next to them was a priest holding a bible in one hand and blessing the patient on the bed. He approached the bed he sighted his mother peacefully sleeping wearing a white nightgown. He recalled the moment of him traveling in the car of Mr. and Mrs. Walsh and recalled the incident of Mrs. Walsh telling her husband how much she will miss her sister. She turned towards James telling him "I know you miss mother James, and I miss her too—but I can promise you everything will be fine, do you understand?" While watching his response giving an assuring smile as James doubtingly nodded.

The party was going on with music playing in the background, the children playing, and the adults busy mingling and laughing.

James whispered "The coast is clear" to give a bit of encouragement to himself looking at the back door from the bottom of the staircase with a suitcase in his hands. It was a cold and a late evening and our story begins on a windy and dull Friday as James turns the doorknob to find the adventure of his own. But as he understood the searching for an adventure was not in a forest but was a name of a place he could reach if he takes the bus stop passing the town through the shortcut in the woods. James wanted to meet her mother's best friend to ask if she knows anything about the Pinnacle, and her friend Suzanne lived quite far and miles away from where James lives.

He planned to not travel directly through the town to take the bus, but through the shortcut in the woods to get the bus to get to where her mother's friend was living. He did not want anyone who knows Mr. and Mrs. Walsh to recognize him. If he gets caught, James knew he will be in great trouble, and Mr. Walsh locks him in the dusty attic for hours as a punishment for the trouble caused before. Whenever nobody is looking James has been trying out his hidden powers to grab things and move things that could be reached from the window with little tree branches without ever touching them. The punishment could be way more for running away than breaking something in the house like one of Mrs. Walsh's crystal collections carried by a small tree branch by trying out his hidden powers. Maybe a few extra hours or a day perhaps in that dark at the dusty attic.

James left the house and kept staggering into the cold woods, and after some time he could feel the slightly heavy suitcase is now a bit heavier than before as his hand is tired of holding the weight of his belongings. The dark and cold forest is full of tall pine trees with the tip of the trees grown into the air and almost invisible as it gets day gets darker turning the Yale blue color light to an Aegean awaiting to get even darker. The ground is uneven with rocks, slopes, and roots of the pine trees grown passing the surface of the ground.

He stopped walking and kept the suitcase on the ground blaming himself saying "Oh this is such a dumb idea! I shouldn't have taken the shortcut in the woods knowing it will be dark soon!" He suddenly hears the sound of a pigeon call, and as he looks around he sighted the red pigeon on a tree branch. It was cleaning its feathers from its peak, and James yelled "Hey you… You have to help me to find the way! It was you that brought me the letter, wasn't it? I'm lost—how can I find the pinnacle?"

The bird took off and he saw the most beautiful and the largest wings for a pigeon. It was much larger than an eagle's wings and with glowing bright red feathers. James ran after it trying to follow the bird but it disappeared. He was cold and tired almost to give up, and suddenly he saw a trail of glowing red feathers on the ground leading him towards the left path into the woods. It was the complete opposite direction James wanted to travel for the shortcut to find the bus stop avoiding the town. He curiously followed the trail of the red feathers, and he stood right in front of a stone wall. It was a dead-end and was covered in creepers and wildflowers.

He moved the creepers on the wall and saw a tiny wooden door behind the creepers. It was hidden into creepers and was an old unpolished ragged door. He knocked with two quick knocks and one, repeating it three times as it was instructed on the letter he received. He hears the door being unlocked and a midget man wearing rags and a hat with a grey long beard up to his knees appeared as the door opens. He had two long dark green leaves on the front of his hat as a weird fashion hat and a red pigeon sitting on top of his hat. He looked nothing like a person in the neighborhood or anywhere he could imagine. He looked like he was living in the forest throughout his entire life. He peeped and looked behind James cautiously asking him with a troubled voice "Did anyone see you?"—Are you sure nobody followed you?"

James replied, "No, but who is…." Before he could finish asking his question James was grabbed from his grey coat from the stomach which was the best reach for the little man and pulled into the little cottage through the stone door frame. The house was dusty with spider webs and everything was small in size matching the little man, the furniture, the old brick stove to the pots and pans. The old man lived in a small cozy and mysterious small cottage-like house that no one could know anyone could be living behind the dead-end camouflaged with climber plants and wildflowers.

James turned around to the old man and asked "Who are you? What is this place? Why are you hiding?"
The man exclaimed "What did you say, lad? —Hiding!"
"I don't hide from anyone eh! I have no such thing as fear with the power of cosmos!"
James replied confusingly "Power of cosmos? Who are you?"
The man answered with his gruff mature voice "I am Mose the gatekeeper, and you must be James from the Spinner family. I was expecting you since two days ago!"
James asked surprisingly "But how do you know my name? — is it you who sent me the letter?" Mose replied with an annoyed look on his face "Listen now, lad— I don't have time to answer all your questions eh!"
Mose took his hand saying "Come now…Hurry — we don't have much time eh!"
The old man wobbling in front of him and took James to a spot covered with gold sand on the wooden floor. He picked up a handful of the glowing sand and poured it into James's palm.
Mose spoke in a commanding voice "Now listen carefully, lad — you have to say Aries raferogus, and as soon as you say it, throw the sand towards your feet but clearly say the name Aries if not—well you will be in a place you wish never to land! Do you understand?"
James nodded and took a deep breath and said the words loudly "Aries raferogus," and threw the sand towards his shoes. In a flash, a bright light appeared and all he knew is that he is now in a completely different place. He was still carrying his suitcase and he checked himself to see if he is in one piece having to go through such a strange way of traveling. He looked around the strange place confused and he recognized the surrounding was nothing like the place before or inside that stone wall he found in the woods.

Chapter Two: Welcome to the Phrontistery

In a flash from the midget man's house was in a place like a paradise with grass, flowers, mountains, and trees all around. He felt a nice cool breeze and saw the fireflies flying all over the place giving a magical sparkle to the moonlight paradise. He sees a shadow of someone walking towards him slowly from afar and watches the person getting closer and closer. It is a woman who looks like a dream or an illusion kind floating as she walks with her bare feet towards him. She stood right in front of him, and he saw her face and body was skin like no other but with the texture of a tree trunk. She wore a cloak made with dried leaves, and from her knees to her ankles were all leaves. The leaves were moving graciously, and as she walks the leaves were moving with her like to a rhythm with the movement of her feet.

She spoke in the most soft and echoing voice saying "Welcome James— I was eager to meet you! My name is Gelda and I will take you to the Phrontistery. You will meet some wonderful friends there!" It was more like a living walking tree that talks and James were in a chaotic moment to utter a word.

He looked at her from head to toe and asked her "Are you a person?" Gelda slightly smiled and replied in her calm soft voice "Oh no! I am the spirit of the forest." James spoke with a quavering voice "Spirit? —so you are a ghost!"

Gelda replied "There is no need to be frightened James—there are two kinds here at the Pinnacle. The spirit pixies of the cosmos like myself —we are protectors of the land—and the great enchanters and enchantresses blessed with the source powers to do great things like you. You will learn everything with time."

James was taken to a town simply magical but walkthrough of a medieval town or place. There were different kinds of spirit pixies wearing long cloaks made out of dried leaves, flowers, and roots. There were also ordinary children and adults but they were all in long black robes like warlocks. The colored clothing was only the cloaks and capes, and the adults were wearing colored cloaks with different symbols on them while the children were wearing purple, blue, and green capes.

The people were busy shopping, walking, and chatting no different from a busy and crowded old age town. He passed little book shops, jewelry stores with living white clay dummies without any features displaying the jewelry were moving and showing off the items like models. Fruits, vegetable shops, and pastries are all crowded with people choosing fruits, buying cakes, pastries, and bread. The buildings were made out of fine wood and some with stack stones, and some decorated with beautiful flowers and plants. James was curiously observing the magical surrounding with the people all around, and suddenly he noticed something significant worn by all the adults—which was a long silver chain that holds a pendant like stone, and the pendant was a round yellowish and glowing. He looked at the pendants closely worn by the people passing by him and noticed some stones were changing colors, pictures, and symbols. It was like a stone with life worn by the ones wearing cloaks. He looked at the stone with amusement and people were passing by looking at his face slightly confused for his stare.

He asked Gelda "What are those pendants people are wearing?"
She replied with great willingness to explain "That is the most important blessing to work with your powers. It is called the power stone, and you will be given one after you learn to use your powers and master them with your learnings —the power stone will be something very valuable to you! It defines who you are as an enchanter."
James and Gelda arrived at a place to an enormous building surrounded by a metal fence that looks highly secured from anyone entering without permission. The building looks like an old library or museum made with dark stones, and with two tall dragon statues on either side of the massive metal gates partially opened to enter. James noticed one of the towers of the building which was slightly towards the left side from the entrance and placed facing in a way of somewhere center of the town when looked from afar. On the very top of the tower was the largest ancient water clock ever made in history. It was beautifully crafted crystal glass with wood-crafted numbers filled with a thick gold liquid that showed the time from anywhere in the town.

Four big flags were waving with pride on the roof of the large entrance door of the building. The center flag was with a red background in a white outlined circle and inside the circle was a white outlined equilateral triangle. The three parts of the triangle had an initial in every portion which was the letter "A" in silver on the first, "W" in blue on the second, and the letter "E" in green on the third. The flag was placed much higher than the rest of the flags, and the remaining three flags look the same except the background in red and had only one letter in the triangle instead of three as in the equilateral triangle. Flag with the grey outline triangle inside the circle in white had the letter "A" in grey with the red background, the flag with a "W" in blue in the blue outlined triangle, and the flag with an "E" in green in the green triangle. James recalled the colors of the capes the children were wearing in the town match the colors of the triangles in the flags.

There was a long line of students wearing ordinary clothes and shoes just like him from the gates to the building. The line was moving quite fast and he saw a man and an old lady wearing black robes calling out names and checking a list. He was watching everything astound to understand what was happening around him, and he heard Gelda telling him with her soft voice in the background

"You have arrived at the Phrontistery and you will be able to manage from here — if you need any assistance I am sure the staff of Phrontistery will help you. I wish you blessings to learn with the boundless knowledge to unlock your powers!" He turned around to speak to Gelda with his thoughts muddled with the surrounding, but she was nowhere and there was no sight of her. He unsurely entered the gates and joined the line like the rest of the children. They were of different ages who are probably from different parts of the world.

He saw a girl a few feet away staring at him. She had long beautiful dark blond hair and brown eyes walked up to him with a warm smile. She introduced herself holding out her hand saying "Hi! I am Laura, nice to meet you."

James smiled back and replied, "Hi, I am James—James Spinner" with a firm handshake.

The girl was looking shocked with the most surprised look on her face "You are James Spinner! Your mother — your mother is Mrs. Joanna Spinner, isn't it? Wow! I read so much about her" Laura said excitedly.

James was surprised with the unexpected response "You knew my mother? James asked highly surprised.

Laura laughed and said "Of course silly—who wouldn't know Mrs. Joanna Spinner! She was one of the greatest enchantresses.

They heard the woman who was checking the list calling out her name with a matured voice "Miss Laura Wilson!" She turned to James "That's me!" and stepped in front of the line. The woman looked up at Laura walking towards her and peeked to look at James standing in line and whispered something to the old man next to her. She checked the list and cried out "Mr. James Spinner!" She announced the name and every student standing in front of him turned around with amusement and peeking to have a glimpse of James. He felt uncomfortable being the center of attention without even knowing what is that special about his name and how he is familiar to others around him when everyone and everything was just too new to him.

The old woman was wearing a black robe and hat with a net covering her face, and a long chain that holds the power stone. She had dark brown and gray hair tied at the back of her head like a bun. She looked slim, and average in height, and the man next to her was old and tall than an average male. He wore a black robe and a bright white cloak, and gray long hair with a well-trimmed gray beard around his mouth. The man had sharp features and looked straight at James and said calmly yet sternly "You are late! We expected your arrival two days ago—anyway—Darwin will show you the way and assist you with your belongings."

He looked at Darwin that looks like a tiny creature indistinguishable from a green Christmas elf wearing dark green rags. It has a nose that shapes like a carrot on a snowman, ears like an elf that has a texture of a leaf, and a skinny body except for his small hanging belly. Darwin looked at him with humble eyes bowing his head
"Greeting sire! Please follow me, I will take you to the assembly room." It had a funny little walk with its long green feet tottering from left to right he takes his steps.

There were mammoth-sized two-spirit pixies that look like knights holding long spears in one hand and a metal shield on the other. The top half of the two-spirit pixies were strong men worn like soldiers with a bottom half of the body and legs that look like an elephant standing on either side of the tall double door fully opened which were covered with creepers with an enormous gold door handle. James followed Darwin through the doors and walked into the building.

They walked through a long doorway and into a large hall that looks like a lobby. The roots go all the way from the bottom of the walls and across the ceilings were decorated with tree roots and floating light drops glowing with a bright yellow light on the ceilings. The light drops were white transparent flower buds, and there was no logical reason whatsoever to have lights in flower buds that floats or moves on their own. There were statues made out of limestone of enchanters and enchantresses with long cloaks, and statues of different spirit pixies with climber plants on them sculptured neatly with every little detail kept on the sides of the walls. The limestone creepers grow and move around the statue like a living plant. James passed looking at one statue of an enchanter wearing a long cloak, hat and robe holding a sculptured fire lamp in one hand. As he looked at the statue it looked down at James greeting him with a polite hat tip. Students around the place were wearing robes and capes walking around the place into different hallways and holding books with covers made out of wood.

Darwin took James to a long desk that looks like an extensive reception table made with polished dark stones. There were six old women elves wearing black Cotehardie gowns seated in the six counters. There were wooden boards above each counter that says what service the particular counter provides such as check-in, student resources, information counter, complaints, administration, power stone registrations/ renewal. Darwin went to the check-in counter and the reception elf lady gave a blank piece of wood plank that's the size of a book page. Darwin turned around to James holding out the wood plank.
"Please place your hand on the wood and tell you're good name sire!" Darwin humbly requested and James placed his hand and uttered his name "James Spinner" and looked up at Darwin. He noticed the elves' attention turning to James as soon they heard his name. The wooden plank engraved his palm print with his name appearing at the bottom of the palm print. Darwin handed over the plank to the counter and took him to a hall with a crowd of students who probably seems new to the place as him. They were busy chattering and mingling with each other, and seem to be the newly enrolled who were wearing casual ordinary clothes. They surely seem familiar with the place while James was trying to absorb everything that he never

expected. The room looks like a chapel except it had roots on the ceiling which was grown to a design that connects to the center of the roof that hangs a long and heavy chandelier nothing less than a designed masterpiece. The chandelier was made with tree roots and decorated with vast glowing flower buds that glow lighting the entire room. The most magical part of the design is the huge flow of water falling from the center of the chandelier that flows down and disappears halfway from the roof. The floor seems fully dry and students were standing underneath the water flower without a single drop of water on them. James kept staring at the chandelier mesmerized and was only back to his right consciousness when Darwin's voice distracted him.

"This is the assembly room—let me take your bag sire, and I will keep it at the quarter entrance" Darwin uttered with his low humble voice.

James handed Darwin the suitcase saying "Thank you, Darwin!"

Darwin was so pleased to hear the polite expression "Oh you're welcome sir. I am always at your service!"

Darwin turned around to leave from the assembly room carrying the suitcase, and paused for a second, to turn back at James uttering "It is truly an honor to meet you sire—and I knew your mother— Dame Joanna Spinner... She was very kind to me!"

Darwin looked down sadly saying "She used to give me fruits and sweets as a kind gesture." He looked back at James with eyes almost to tear saying "Her death is a great loss for all of us sire—she was talented at the same time the kindest."

Before James could respond, a sound of a throat clearing is heard in the background. Darwin's sad face suddenly changes to a frightened look by looking at someone behind James and quickly runs away. James looked around and it was a tall heavy built man with a bald head somewhere in his fifties looking down at him with a slight smile.

The man greeted saying "Hello" and walked past him through the crowd to the front of the room. He stepped on the wooden deck made in front of the massive stained-glass window of the room and looked at the students with a polite smile. He was wearing a black robe and a red cincture. James stood right at the back of the crowd looking at the man on the wooden deck. He was wearing like a priest and seems friendly with a wide smile but seems to be a pan am smile for some reason.

Through the crowd, Laura appeared walking towards James "Hey James! I was looking for you— I want you to meet my friends this is Henry and Mathew." James looked at the two students standing next to her.

They were one tall and one average, Mathew had. "Hi, nice to meet you!" James said politely smiling at both of them.

"Hi, there! Nice to meet I'm Henry—Henry Davis." said the one that had dark brown hair and dark brown eyes

"This is my brother Mathew." Henry said with a friendly impression showing his brother with dark bronze wavy hair cut to a bob with dark brown eyes, and the one taller. Mathew smiled and seems to have a pleasing personality just like his brother.

"Hi James, a pleasure to meet you!"

He had a bit of a deeper voice than Henry but polite tone of voice. James noticed Laura looking at Mathew with a slight smile, and it was obvious she likes him.

A bit far from where they were standing James noticed a girl at a distance looking at him between Henry and Mathew. She had red curly hair with blue eyes, wearing a blue dress that brings out the color of her eyes perfectly and an orange scarf, stockings with shoes to match her attire looking away as soon as he smiled.

Henry was looking at them all along and said "Ah… the little miss quiet!"

James looked at Henry and asked with a casual voice "Do you know her?"

"Oh yes! Her name is Marie Jones and she is related to us, well a distant relative actually from our father's side! Henry replied calmly. "We all meet for Christmas, family gatherings, and things, but she doesn't talk much. She is a bit shy and reserved I suppose." Said, Henry.

Mathew grunted with a sarcastic tone "More like ego if you ask me!"

A matured woman's voice occurred in the background "Okay everyone! Silence please."

The room is more calm and silent with Henry, Mathew, Laura, and James all faced to the front of the room to pay attention along with the rest of the students. It was the lady who was checking the list wearing a black hat and a net covering her face at the entrance into the Phrontistery. The tall old man who was standing next to her at the entrance and two other men wearing black robes, one wearing a blue cloak and the other a brown cloak walked behind them joining the bald man who was already standing on the wooden deck.

The old man with a white cloak stepped forward and loudly announced with his stern voice. "Greetings, and welcome to the Phrontistery! We are the lecturers and the examination panel. I am Professor Galdor the president of the faculty and from this day forward you will be students of the Phrontistery learning to be great enchanters and enchantresses—there will be no difference from where you are or your backgrounds— as the students of the Phrontistery we consider all equal!"

There is a cloth backdrop hanging from the ceiling that stops above two feet from the wooden deck, and all of a sudden a badge appeared on the backdrop and it had a typical academic badge shape with the logo of the white circle and the three letters inside the equilateral triangle which was on the flag that was at the top of the building.

Professor Galdor looked carefully and announced in a gravelly voice yet loud enough for everyone around the room.

"You will be provided with your lecture schedules by professor Cuppins and all other information that you will need for your daily routine at the faculty! This is the logo of the faculty and the symbol that represents all of you and your power sources which are Water, Air, and last but not least Earth."

While he mentioned the three power sources the symbol on the cloth changed to the blue triangle logo as he mentioned Water, green for Earth, and purple for Air.

He continued explaining in his deep mature voice "You will be allowed to take a sip from the wisdom cup and it will tell you the source power you are gifted to hold. You will be allocated to a congress and its quarters after your source power is identified and announced at the welcoming feast—where you will be able to get to know your fellow students. The congresses are named Adam's Ale, Gravel, and Welkin respectively! So we shall see you all at the welcoming feast in about an hour and Professor Cuppins our vice president will advise you on the rules and regulations and every important detail you will need to know."

He smiled at the students and looked at Professor Cuppins as she nodded slightly smiling back thanking for the address. He stepped down from the wooden deck as his white cloak brushed the wooden floor and walked out of the entrance graciously.

Professor Cuppins stepped forward and said with a glance at the students from left to right and right to left then center through the black net covering her face.

"Welcome students! My name is Andreastea Cuppins and I teach the scientific disciplines that involve both theory and practical sessions. Your lecture schedule will be provided in your quarters along with your uniforms, stationery, and student handbook which will provide further information on your subjects and examinations as well as the faculty rule book. Students cannot leave the faculty without prior permission from the respective lecturer or a faculty head during the lecture hours. The lectures start at eight thirty in the morning and a lunch break at twelve for an hour. Evening sessions will be till three thirty, and your punctuality and discipline will be closely monitored. We expect students to arrive at the dining room right on time to avoid any delays to attend your lectures. Breakfast will be served at seven thirty and dinner at six, post-dinner all students are requested to be in your respective quarters sharp by nine."

The students were looking quite surprised for the strict set of rules and professor Cuppins looked around with a lopsided grin and uttered in a sarcastic voice "The rules set by the faculty is strict but once you are a post-graduate after the fourth year—you will be more relaxed and independent! In your senior years, you will be gathering your postgraduate knowledge on mastering your power stones. You will also be enrolled in our internship programs that will be provided by our faculty to areas of your interests."

The students were beaming at each other excited with the faculty have to offer while James was still lost as he was only expecting to catch a bus to meet her mother's friend Suzanne.

Professor Cuppins introduced a male spirit pixie that just floated from the entrance and into the assembly room stopping close to the wooden deck. He was wearing a robe and partially transparent with a flounce of the robe blended into the thin air like a cloud of smoke. He had a calm oval shape face and long braided hair which was floating behind him and moving on its own. "Now! This is Phanto, and you will be assisted by Phanto to find the way to your quarters. If you sight Phanto and need a direction to a class or a place you are supposed to be— you may ask for assistance."
Professor Cuppins looked around at the students seeing the unsure faces "Go on now!" she said encouraging the students to leave with Phanto.

The students followed Phanto as he floated out of the room and lead the students through the hallway that had shadows of pigeons flying all over the walls. They passed an area that had a water fountain that looks like a true waterfall surrounded by a breathtaking landscape of flowers and plants with a tiny fairy spirit pixie flying around waving at the students. Passing the fountain were two stairways to get to either side of the upper floor with the stairs and the finely crafted railings made with polished wood, and a stair runner carpet made with red feathers. They walked up the staircase and to a huge hall that had four doors two on one side and two on the opposite side of the hall. After each door was a huge face with eyes closed molded faces on the stone wall with the remaining walls on the two sides had shadows of birds flying on the stack stone walls. The ceiling was the usual as the lobby with floating light drops and roots.

There were big wooden boxes stacked one after another along the wall with names engraved in front of each box. "Hey… This box has my name on it!" A boy among the student said loudly and excitedly.
"Here are the essentials that you will need—you are given a set of robes and capes will be provided after allocating you to the congress in the welcoming feast. You will be given a set of clothing every year and during your lecture hours till dinner, you should be dressed only in uniforms. You may dress in your casual

attire post eight in the late evening, and tomorrow stay here prepared for your first day sharp eight after breakfast for a tour of the faculty." Phanto announced with his smooth voice most calmly.

The students rushed towards the boxes grabbing the box under their names eager to look inside the box. It had robes and ten notebooks with wooden covers, two pairs of polished black shoes, two red sweaters, and a piece of red paper with a handwritten note saying

"Welcome to the Phrontistery and on behalf of the faculty management, staff, undergraduate and post-graduate committee we want to wish you good luck, and may the powers of the great universe and Aries be with you throughout the years!"

Chapter Three: Rattle of the Spirit Dragon

The wisdom mug had a crafted face with every little detail that looks nothing less of a realistic man's face with a full beard and straight hair that falls on the sides and around the mug. The thing looks like a fine crafted ornamental mug except for the clay mug talks, hears, sees as it speaks when the students take a sip of some never finishing water in the mug.

 "Rob Weng in the power of earth, ground, plants and every seed of the soil, you belong to the congress of Gravel number one hundred and four" The mug uttered in its sophisticated voice. Mathew had his turn and he belongs to Adam's Ale— he turned around to James saying in an excited voice "You're next James!"

The lecturers wearing robes and different colored cloaks were seated at the head table. Professor Galdor was looking closely at James. Some of them were gathering their eyebrows and others including Professor Cuppins and Professor Galdor were both looking curiously at James as he walked up to the head table and picked up the wisdom cup to have a sip.

The mug uttered "Oh my golly gosh! It's him— Spinner! Let's see the best seems to be Gravel but this does not satisfy enough with the power you are blessed with—oh well—number one hundred and seventeen" James looked at the mug in his hand confused as he looked at the lecturers who were staring at him with a pleasing look.

It must be the finest feast table with rows and rows of spirit pixies wearing red waiter coats and black trousers who were floating with dishes of poultry, meats, bread, pastries, fruits, sweets, and desserts serving the long tables. The tables and benches are made with wood and a long table runner made with red flower petals with floating lights on the ceilings that look like a grand ballroom in a fairy tale. Utensils, plates, and bowls are all made with wood and the glass water goblets for each plate are crafted with a detail-rich design.

Laura and James are both in Gravel, Mathew and his brother Henry both in Adams Ale. They were taken by the head students of the congresses to the quarters who are in the third year of the undergraduate years wearing the black robes, capes according to colors of the respective congress but a gold V line on the front and back of the capes connecting on the shoulders that represent their position of a head student of the congress. On their way to the congress, Laura catches up to James pacing through the crowd.

"James do you have any memories of your mother?" asked Laura.

"Yes but very few, I wish I had though— I miss her!" James replied calmly.

"Oh, I am sorry James, I didn't mean to upset you." Laura replied apologetically and James looked at Laura asking doubtfully "How much do you know about my mother Laura?"

"Oh, she was the greatest and the best—She was magnificent and I've heard and read so much about her from the articles and…" She replied going on with great excitement.

James interrupted her complimenting the greatness of his mother saying "I mean about my mother's death— do you know anything about it and what happened to her?"

Laura looked around with a worried expression whispering "Let's get to the quarters first and I'll tell you!"

James was curious to know what she knew with her response. They headed towards the quarter doors. The head student said their names standing in front of the stone faces on the walls, and a wooden plank came out from the mouth of the stone face right next to the quarter door. The three head students' place their palms on the palm print on the wood. The head student pushes the wooden plank back into the mouth of the stone face on the wall and the door opens to the quarters recognizing the palm print of the head student.

There was a long row of beds on either side of the room made with roots and a pillow cover made life of a huge leaf. A boy next to him looked at his bed and pillow commenting sarcastically "How on earth will this be comfortable?" he jumped onto the bed and relaxed saying "I can sleep on this forever… This is great!" There was a narrow door next to each hood of the bed, and James walked up to the door with the number one hundred and seventeen" and opened the door slowly stepping into the small room. It had a wardrobe, a stone bathtub on the corner, and water flowing from the ceiling to the water-filled bathtub that never overflows. It's just too magical for James to sight, and he saw his suitcase was kept right next to his wardrobe. Next to the wardrobe, there was a water puddle in a perfect rectangle shape, but strangely the puddle is on the wall that gives a clear reflection same as a mirror. He opened his cupboard and there were some folded new green capes with a hanger made with plant strings hanged on the pole inside the wardrobe. On top of the second shelf was the lecturer schedule on a wooden plank piece that had subjects such as science, history, arts, philosophy, and classics

The girls' dormitory was on the other side of the wall on the far corner that had its stone frame entrance leaded by the pathway between the two rows of beds of the boys quarter. Laura walked out of the entrance and towards James.

"Let's go to the study room, there will be fewer students there!" Laura uttered while she walked out of the congress quarter doors.

They sat on of the wooden stools in the round study tables, and there were large study lamps fixed to the floor that reaches above the table and bent to the center of the table. Each lamp is covering the whole table by the massive flower-shaped lamp underneath.

"I will tell you what I know but I do not prefer to talk about it openly—do you understand?" As she watched his response closely.

James nodded looking at her awaiting curiously to hear what she knows.

"Your mother was known as the enchantress of the spirit dragon—the only enchanter who had the power to summon and control the dark powers of the witchcraft."

"Spirit dragon?" James asked curiously.

"Yes! The dragon spirit is the father of fire and it is the most powerful than any of the power sources. The witchcrafts uses the power stone of the spirit dragons and legends say the stone is hidden somewhere in the dark hills!"

"Where is it?" James asked Laura.

"No one knows where the dark hills are but it is out there—somewhere"

"Have you heard anything about what happened to my mother?" James asked Laura curiously.

Laura looked at James sadly and said softly "There was a rumor saying she was murdered." Laura paused speaking looking worried and speechless.

"What is it, Laura? Please—tell me!?" James cried out looking at her with fearful eyes.

She looked at James and took a deep breath.

 "Burton!" said Laura.

"Burton?" James exclaimed and Laura looked around anxiously to see if anyone heard it.

"Shhhh that name is not allowed within the faculty. It's forbidden to talk about him!" Laura hushed James worriedly.

"Where is Burton now?" James whispered with great anger on his face.

"No one knows where he is or what he looks like, but they say he stole your mother's power stone which was the most powerful than any other power stones of any enchanter or enchantress. They say it is still with Burton, and he awaits to find a way to use the blessings of the stone to unlock the high-powers and take control of the pinnacle of Aries. The power stone cannot be used for any witchcrafts or spells without having the source power of the spirit dragon. The only way you get these source powers are if you're born with it, and—"

Laura suddenly stopped explaining and was staring at James with eyes wide and looking completely shocked.

"What?" James grunted

"The power source—it—it comes from family," Laura replied making a line between her eyebrows. She remained silent lost in deep thought for just a few seconds.

 "James! There is a high possibility that you are born with the source powers of the spirit dragon and you might be at great risk!" Laura said in a low voice concernedly.

"James you have to be careful, since you might be Burton's only hope."

James nodded hiding his fear as he looked at Laura. His face changed from fear to sadness having to remember the words his mother's death was a murder.

Mrs. Cuppins's voice was heard in the background announcing "Attention students! Please go to your quarters and students are not allowed to be out of the quarter doors after nine pm without prior permission. Thank you."

Laura stood up saying "We should get back, see you tomorrow James—Good night!"

"Good night!" James replied calmly.

James was fast asleep and he was dreaming of walking into his mother's bedroom exactly the way he saw her for the last time. She was wearing the sliver nightgown, the two maids and a priest standing around the bed all staring at James without any expressions as he walks into the room. He sees his mother holding a power stone in her hand. The yellow glowing stone had a black smoke oozing inside the stone that covered the yellow stone to black while he was looking. He reached out to take the stone instead he suddenly woke up opening his eyes with great shock, sweaty and breathing heavily hearing the melody of multiple bells ringing. He sat on the bed and looked around seeing the children rushing, getting out of their beds, and ready to start the day.

James was dressed in the black robe, green cape, and finely polished black shoes ready for his first day at the Phrontistery looking at his reflection on the mirror of crystal clear water. James went to the dining room and sees Mathew, Henry, and Laura already seated at the dining table.
"Good morning James!" Mathew said with an energetic voice.
"You're looking good James," Henry said loudly making James feel a bit embarrassed while Laura, Henry, and Mathew giggled.
"You look good too Henry!" James replied.

Laura is eating an apple while Henry is having some cereal, and James reached out to grab a sandwich that was neatly arranged on a long tray. He sees the girl Marie who was looking at him at the assembly room seated on the other side of the long table a few seats away from where they were seated. He noticed that she was wearing a purple cape which means she is in the Welkin congress. She slightly smiled at him but instantly looked away before James could smile back. James sees Mose wobbling with his red pigeon on his hat through the entrance walking towards the separated long table for the spirit pixies a step below the head table and passing James as he walked behind him.

"Hey there!" Mose said having a glance at everyone smiling and giving a small pat on James's back as he passed him.

A girl at the table loudly said, "Good morning Mose!"

"You all look great in that attire but mine is better eh—I prefer mine more stylish with holes, stains, and fine details! Mose said in a sarcastic voice making everyone laugh at his hilarious comment.

Professor Cuppins and the lecturer who looks like a priest walked into the long dining room and everyone was silent and settled.

"Good morning students! There is an announcement for the second-year students—please note your grades including the feedback of your projects are released to your report books." Announced Professor Cuppins.

James confusingly looked at Laura, Mathew, and Henry.

"How can grades be released to a book?" James asked.

"What do you mean? Asked Henry after gulping down a spoonful of milk and cereal from the bowl.

"How is it normal to release grades and feedback to a book?" James asked taking a bite from his sandwich.

Laura giggled softly replying "Don't expect things to be normal here James!"

Mathew nodded to agree with Laura as they all started tittering but was also the simple truth.

James, Henry, Mathew, and Laura were seated in their first lecture which is history, and the bald lecturer wearing like a priest walked into the classroom.

"Hello everyone! Good morning to all of you and I am professor Tolmen and I teach history—which is also your very first session in the Phrontistery! You may call me Father Tolmen, and I am also the priest and spirit guide in the faculty."

He looked around the class smiling and gathering his hands together.

"Students please open your notebooks and write down your names and your respective congress." Father Tolmen instructed calmly.

James opened the wooden cover book and found a blue feather which was inside the book.

James took the feather but nowhere could he find an ink bottle.

"How can we write without ink?" asked James from Laura who was seated next to him.

"You don't need any silly!"

 She took the feather inside her book and wrote her name and "Gravel" in brackets on the inner cover of her book. The feather writes just perfect in blue ink without needing a single dip of the feather point to an ink bottle.

James looked at the feather fully amazed and wrote his full name on the inner cover of his book.

"Neat!" James uttered in an excited little voice.

"Can anyone tell me the name of our land? The Pinnacle of what do they call it?" Asked Father Tolmen, and almost every hand was up with confidence to answer. Father Tolmen pointed to a girl in the front row on the left.

"The Pinnacle of Aries!" Answered the girl,

"Excellent!" replied Father Tolmen.

A reception elf lady walked in pulling a wooden cart filled with five tall piles of brown hardcover books into the classroom.

"Thank you Doris!" replied Father Tolmen to the elf lady. She pulled the cart to the front and a corner dropping the handle of the cart on the floor. She did not smile or look at anyone and was fully engaged at the task wobbling back out of the classroom.

"Here—keep one for yourselves and pass down the rest to others." Professor Tolmen instructed giving a set of books to all the students in the front row to pass the books to the back until there were no more books remaining in the cart.

"These are your textbooks—Turn to page ten once you receive your copy."

James kept a book for himself and passed the rest of the books to Henry who was seated behind him. The book looks new with the title "History of Aries (Volume one)".

Father Tolmen walked around the class slowly as he started the lesson saying

"History is always a mystery and until you know how things began—you will be like a lost being, and so

lost to a point you will not know where you are no matter how much you see or hear around you!" He looked

at James as he was passing with the sort of expression that was said exactly to James.

He walked to the front and center of the class

"Aries was powerful and also known as the god of love and peace. A great warrior who fought for goodness

and justice of the universe. Aries had a son which we call the spirit dragon—there is not much to say about

the spirit dragon." He said in a calm voice.

James and Laura looked at each other with both knowing there is much more importance and history that is

personal to James. He is still surprised his mother had the source powers of such superior that's being

considered as a legend in history.

Father Tolmen continues distracting James from his thoughts

"The Trophen witchcraft tribe fought with Aries to gain the source powers of the universe. Aries fought for

justice and peace with the Trophen tribe that uses dark witchcraft—the source powers make the dark

witchcrafts very powerful and undefeatable."

He started walking about the class explaining the history with students listening with great interest to know

how it all began.

"The source powers are known as the high-powers of the universe and therefore Aries fought and defeated

the Trophen witchcraft tribe with the spirit dragon. Aries has gifted land with spirit pixies as protectors and

with the most important gift—the source powers! The three source powers are Water presented for the

selfless love towards the universe and safety of the people, Air for courage, and earth for wisdom. Aries

picked two ordinary people after searching the entire universe for the evolution of source power and its

generations. Aries chose two children who were orphans than two adults who could use and expose the

source powers with the ordinary human world. The children grew up in the land—the land we call the

Pinnacle of Aries. One of them fell in love with a spirit pixie called the Spirit of mortal—the protector of the power sources, while the other joined the Trophen witchcraft. All of us learning to be enchanters and enchantresses are from the generations born by the unity of the spirit of mortal and one of the humans chosen by Aries."

Father Tolmen walked up to the wooden board that's made with the fine wood of a cut to the middle of a strong tree trunk. Picking up a piece of chalk in the wooden pen holder on the table.
"Now I will write some questions on the board, and I want you to write them down on your notebooks and answer— you may read page ten to page sixteen in your textbooks and I want complete answers to the questions. I will give you exactly thirty minutes!" Starting to write on the board with a feather and erased the board with a leaf just like good old blackboard chalk and duster.

James is a very hard worker and the more he learned about the powers he had, the more he wanted to study them. He felt free and enjoyed every minute of it with his new friends Laura, Mathew, and Henry. It's being almost a month but Marie is still uncomfortable to speak with any of them apart from just a slight smile. She always keeps to herself and loves to draw and sketch portraits and landscapes. She enjoys sketching on paper or behind her notebooks as she sits on the benches in the garden during her free time. Laura is a book worm and she gets lost in the world of books on history or autobiography books of great enchanters and enchantresses. There are times she reads novels and weeps silently as she is being captured with the emotions of the story. Henry and Mathew have a great sibling relationship, and they do argue a bit or debate with each other but they are more like friends than brothers. They spend their free time either studying or playing chess or various kinds of board games. James practices his powers with trees and sculpting with his powers to bend or break rocks and smoothening with another rock and trying out many things on his textbooks and what he learns in his classes. He takes over the kindness and the good heart after his mother to be kind towards Darwin, the helper elf. They all have a great time during classes playing tricks on each other, and James is now more adapted to the strangeness of the place.

It was a long day for James and he had his dinner as usual, and he was fast asleep in his bed. It was heavily raining outside and he heard a sound of a rattle. He panicked jumping out of the bed thinking it's a rattlesnake and probably somewhere near him. The boy in the bed next to him was peacefully sleeping, but James heard the sound again clear and close as if it was right next to him. He took a step back startled and knocked on the bed next to him waking up the boy.

"Hey… Come on James — Go back to sleep!" The boy said in a sleepy voice.

James wanted to ask him if he hears the sound of a rattle, but the boy was sleeping while softly snores with his mouth open. James used his powers and pulled a light drop from the roots on the ceiling and checked if his bed was all clear. He went back to bed, and again the rattle sound kept coming over and over. He covered his ears with his pillow to avoid hearing the loud rattle sound.

James had the usual morning routine and all the students were rushing to their scheduled lectures. Harry and Mathew were walking behind James and Laura chatting away and laughing carried away in their conversations.

They were walking down the hallway turning right and up the staircase to another hallway, and turned right then left passing the magical walls with dripping waterfalls, ones with climber plants moving around with blooming flowers that change colors and texture, and the neatly build stack stone walls with shadows of a flock of pigeons flying all over the walls.

"I got something to tell you!" said James looking at Laura with a nervous look on his face.

"What is it, James?" Laura asked casually.

"Last night I heard a rattling sound, and I thought it was a rattlesnake and…."

 "A rattlesnake?" Laura interrupted replying suddenly.

"Yes, but I don't know where it came from!" James replied with frowning his eyebrows.

Laura suddenly stopped walking and James, Henry, and Mathew all stood confusingly.

"What's up Laura? Are you okay?" Mathew asked.

"The spirit dragon!" Laura mumbled looking at James with eyes wide and shocked.

"What?" Mathew and James asked together with Laura's unexpected response. Laura said with a compelling voice "Let's get to the library—now!"

Laura turned a page of a thick history book in the library, and she ran her finger while she reads the passage. "The spirit dragon or the Father of fire is the only son of Aries. He can fight with the power of thunder and great powers with the source of fire which is also the most dangerous and powerful source of power that can be used to strengthen dark witchcraft. Only the son of Aries received the power and was hidden for the safety of the people and to protect them from anyone misusing it. The spirit dragon has a large pigeon's face, dragon wings with red feathers on the face, neck, and wing. The rest of the body especially the tail is a rattlesnake, and the legend says that a call of the spirit dragon is hearing a clear sound of a rattle."
 She turned to the next page but two pages were torn off from the book.
"Seems like someone had torn the pages," said James softly making sure no one around hears him.
"Maybe whoever tore the pages did not want anybody to know what's in those two pages!" Henry said looking at James and Laura full of curiosity.

James, Laura, Mathew, and Henry came running into the class, and all the students turned around to look at them. Professor Cuppins narrowed her eyes looking at the latecomers through the net slightly bowing down her head and looking mostly at James.
"You are late!" She said like a steaming teapot.
"Sorry Professor Cuppins," said Laura walking into the classroom while the others apologized after her as they sat on the very last row which was the only set of available seats left.
During class the four facing the lecturer trying to absorb her teaching, but their minds were somewhere else, somewhere worrying.
"What are we going to do now?" whispered Mathew to James.
"We got to find a clue—one way or another!" James replied with great determination with Laura and Henry and Mathew feeling the most righteous thing to do.

Chapter Four: The Warning

James, Laura, Henry, and Mathew were studying outside in the courtyard in a bright sunny day, all seated on the trimmed green grass with little green elves trimming the flower bushes on the far edge of the courtyard. A group of students walked towards them and seems to be maybe a year or two senior to them. "Well—well—well it's the talk of the town Mr. James Spinner!'' said the boy right in front of the group. All of them in different congresses wearing capes and the boy who made the sarcastic comment is a reddish-blond with hazel eyes and pale skin. He was one of the tallest from the group with a smug kind of smile wearing a cape of the Gravel congress. He got close to James and bent down to look closely grabbing from his robe. "Don't you try to be some star here James—do you understand? Just know your limits Spinner and you will be fine!" the boy said staring furiously with his dark hazel eyes with an envious voice.

"Leave them alone Wilbert!" a command came somewhere at the back of the senior group. They all looked back and it was Professor Fyn Sisko, who wears a blue cloak with a symbol of two white drama masks with one happy and one sad. He has silver hair and is styled like a nineteen eighties musician hairstyle and a Balbo beard. He teaches arts including music, sculpting, art, writing, poetry and opera belonging to the Welkin congress with a knowledge of highly mastered powers and a multi-talented enchanter in creativity.

"Go back to your classes —and you better get on with your exam pieces—I do not entertain anyone with half practiced and unprepared in my class! He said to the senior students as they walked away fast but very reluctantly looking back at James especially Wilbert.

"James, you're okay?" Professor Sisko asked with his agile and soft voice as he walked towards him.

"Yes! Thank you professor Sisko" James replied.

"Oh you're welcome, I shall see you all tomorrow," said Professor Sisko softly with a smile as he walked away.

"Prince just saved your day James!" Henry said sarcastically, and the two brothers laughed.

"Shut up Henry!" Laura responded with a dominant voice.

The bells were ringing to a pleasing melody in the Phrontistery for the next lecture or place they were supposed to attend and they all walked back into the building.

They were in a middle of a biology lecture and James hears the rattle close to his ear. He covers his ears from his palms, as he takes Professor Cuppins's attention. She sights James covering his ears in the middle of her class.

"You heard enough haven't you Mr. James Spinner?" said Professor Cuppins in a sarcastic and displeased voice making the rest of the class laugh at James as he uncovers his ears looking around the classroom.

"I am sorry Mrs. Cuppins!" James replied calmly.

Through the classroom window, James sees Darwin sneaking into the woods and looking around making sure no one sees him. During the lunch hour, James ran out of the building and towards the woods with Laura, Mathew, and Henry following him into the woods.

"James—Wait—where are you going?" Laura asked confusedly.

"It's Darwin—I saw him sneaking into the woods, there is got to be something in there!

They walked into the forest woods with tiny pixie fairies flying all over buzzing like bees.

"Look!" said Mathew pointing at something right next to his feet. It was a track of something large that had slide to the forest twice bigger than a python.

"It looks like a snake track!" Laura said looking closely at the tracks.

"I am not much fond of snakes," Henry said with a stolid look on his face.

James started to walk along the track with the others following him. It leads to a cave behind a waterfall with the water flowing covering the entrance of the cave. The water does not flow anywhere else but just disappears after it hits the surface of the ground.

"Let's go!" said James as he was about to walk through the water and Mathew grabbed James's arm to stop him from stepping any further.

"James we cannot go into the Phrontistery being all soaking wet!" said Mathew as he looked at the water and back at James.

"No! There should be a reason why we were lead to this place—and that rattle sound that I am hearing," James replied with a sense of agitation.

"He kept hearing the rattle sound the moment he walks into the cave dripping water from his hair and clothes with Laura, Henry, and Mathew following him with all their clothes and shoes soaking wet.
The more he walks into the cave, the rattle sound kept getting louder and louder making him run to see what or where it is leading him. They ran to a space in the cave that had a wooden ceiling with beams of sunlight that shoots straight onto the center of the ground. There were red feathers all over the floor and spider webs on the walls that looked like a place that was abandoned ages ago.
"This place looks spooky—we got to go back!" said Henry worriedly as he looks around with a fearful face.
"We got to find out the two pages that were ripped off from the book James—we may find a clue!" said Laura fully determined.
"Laura's right! I too believe there is something that whoever who tore those pages does not want anyone to know!" said Mathew curiously.

They went back to the Phrontistery making a track of water on the floor with their hair and clothes dripping with water. The spirit pixie that passed them wearing a green old robe with frog legs, long nose with green lips passed them looking shocked as they were all covered with water. A man with shoulder-length gray and dark brown hair with a center bald head, a medium-length beard wearing a brown cloak, and with the black printed symbol of a letter in the Greek alphabet like the letter I and an O., He is Professor Conan Lansford who teaches philosophy and classics, a man with strict discipline and an old school mindset highly supportive to Professor Cuppins with disciplinary matters in the faculty. It is the last person they hoped to have to run into when soaking wet after exploring a place they were not supposed to be as per their schedule.

Professor Lansford looked surprised at Laura, Henry, and Mathew from head to toe and frowned when he sees James. "Mr. Spinner and his committee—I see that you have had a wonderful time wondering afar from your schedules. Let's go meet the Vice President of the faculty—I am sure she would love to hear how much you all have been enjoying by skipping your philosophy sessions that are scheduled an hour ago!" He said with his husky and with an arrogant voice.

"I knew we will be in trouble," whispered Henry simply irritated and scared at the consequence.

"Can you please explain yourselves for this unaccepted behavior that I am witnessing?" Said Professor Cuppins with her usual low-pitched voice and displeased.

"We are sorry Professor Cuppins, please forgive us! We—um—we — I tripped and I fell pushing James along with Henry and Mathew to the water fountain near the stairway—It was just an accident and we apologize for the mess! Said Laura with a trembling voice but striving to say with confidence.

"Oh is it? That is quite an accident indeed!" commented Professor Cuppins looking unconvinced with the excuse. Professor Lansford stepped forward looking neutral as he watches them giving shivers to Henry.

 "That would be very convincing Miss Wilson if that is in anyway possible to happen." Professor Lansford said calmly.

Laura, James, Henry, and Mathew all looked surprised with not being able to understand what Professor Lansford meant by speaking about the impossibility of the accident.

"You see — we are in a place with wonders—and we are in a place of high source powers that makes the impossible possible. In the Pinnacle of Aries, the source powers of Adam's Ale represents in all the walls and fountains decorated with water. If you fall or touch the water — It will not get you soaking wet, nor a single drop will be in your skin or clothes — Just like the mirrors in your quarters!" Said Professor Lansford with his husky old voice.

"If you are soaking wet you have either lost your minds to shower yourselves in the bathtubs with your uniforms on during your lectures—or you have to be in a place you are NOT supposed to be! "This is the final warning to all of you— next time you will be taken to Professor Galdor — now go on—change to a dry set of uniforms and get back to your lectures!" Said Professor Cuppins frowning and focusing mostly on James same as Professor Lansford.

It was in the evening and all students in casual attire at the study room with James, Laura, Henry, and Mathew seated on the bean bags made with dried leaves discussing to find a way to know what was in those two torn pages of the book in the library.

"What if we try to get another book outside the faculty? I mean it could be available in books shops outside the Phrontistery." James suggested.

"Well it is a book published by the faculty itself but they could have sent it out to sell in the markets!" replied Laura.

"Nope sorry dearest—there was no bulk printed on that book. There were two books—one for the faculty use, and the other with Professor Galdor! Said the old lady wearing round glasses wearing an early renaissance style gown at the little publishing house near the faculty that looks like an old shack.

"But why just two copies of that book?" asked James from the old lady.

"Some books are only for the faculty reference and facts secured within the Phrontistery." Replied the old lady with her trembling voice looking over her glasses.

"I noticed that the book did not state the author—can you tell us the name of the author?" Asked Laura curiously.

"Well… I'm afraid I cannot tell you that since I am not allowed to—the author name is the Phrontistery and no personal name is disclosed—why are you children so interested about this book anyway?" asked the woman suspiciously.

"It's just such a lovely book!" said Henry with a forceful wide smile.

The woman pretended to be convinced but she looked at James and Laura with great curiosity over her glasses.

They walked back into the quarters from the publishing center and back to the study room. Professor Sisko walks in and sees James, Laura, and the two Davis brothers.

"There is a poetry writing contest at four thirty in the evening at the Spring Valley art room tomorrow, and I am expecting the presence of all four of you!" said Professor Sisko in his soft voice.

"Will be there!" said Laura smiling at professor Sisko as he leaves the study room.

"Poetry? I cannot rhyme two words I tell you!" said Mathew making his brother, James, and Laura smirk. It was evening and all students including the ones who loved to be a part of the contest and the ones who were reluctant to take part like Mathew were seated and ready at the poetry contest. Darwin is distributing papers and a blue feather is kept on every table. The contest started and some contestants writes calmly and full of passion, whereas Mathew has a few cuts and chops the words looking dissatisfied and almost to give up. James was calmly writing without giving much pressure to it and taking it as a moment of relaxation, except when he hears the rattle sound. He couldn't stop hearing and it distracted him completely, as the sound was getting louder and louder. The iris of his eye expanded with an orange circle and a yellow inner circle with a black pupil that resembles a pigeon's eye. His eyes half-closed and started writing four sentences on the paper in some kind of symbols and an unrecognizable language.

He woke up on a bed with a vision blurred and unclear for a few seconds seeing some people surrounding him. As the vision gets clearer he recognizes the people were Professor Cuppins, Professor Galdor, Father Tolmen, Professor Sisko, and a matured looking spirit pixie lady that wore a robe made with long white flower petals. James suddenly sat on the bed confused and saw the lecturers looking at him all surprised and slightly worried.

"Calm down James—you had a faint but you will be fine!" said Professor Galdor holding from his shoulder. However James has a slight memory something strange happened to him as he recalled the loud rattle sound he heard at the Spring Valley art room, and it was certainly more than just a faint.

He looked around the place and it was rows of beds with sheets and pillows all made with white feathers with three spirit pixies wearing uniforms made with long white flower petals one near him, one making the beds and the other pouring liquids from tiny wooden bottles to another. It looks like a hospital student was wearing a robe sleeping a few beds away from him.

James was sat on the bed of the hospital still confused and trying to remember what happened after hearing the loud rattle sound. Laura, Mathew, and Henry arrived with Laura holding a small wooden box.

"How are you James?" asked Henry

"I am fine!" He replied.

"Here—we brought you some cookies since you like them," Laura said giving him the wooden box she was holding.

James looked at Laura, Henry, and Mathew thinking maybe they could tell him what happened.

"What happened to me in the art room?" James asked.

Laura's, Mathew's, and Henry's smiles changed instantly looking worried as they looked at each other without uttering a word.

"Please—tell me!" James said with great agitation in his eyes.

"You wrote the language that's said to be in the powers of the spirit dragon and you were whispering some words we didn't understand," Laura replied.

"How do you know it is the language of the powers of spirit dragon?" James asked curiously.

"Because that is what it is—and the whole faculty knows—everyone is talking about it," said Mathew

"This will not be good with Wilbert for sure!" said Henry in a sarcastic voice.

In the background, a noise of a throat clearing came behind Laura, Henry, and Mathew. They turned around and it was Professor Galdor walking towards them looking calm as usual.

"See you later James!" Laura said leaving the hospital along with Harry and Mathew passing Professor Galdor.

James was seated on the bed looking at Professor Galdor as he sat on the side of the bed looking calmly at James.

"Hello, James! I want to speak to you about something—and I don't want you to be worried since this is strictly between you and me. I want to help you!" said professor Galdor with his deep mature voice. He gave a piece of paper which was the symbols that he wrote at the poetry contest without his consciousness or knowledge. James looked at Professor Galdor worried saying

"Oh, I am sorry sir—I didn't mean to—" Professor Galdor stopped James from apologizing any further.

"James! There is no need to apologize—you are blessed with a unique power that is born rarely to an enchanter or enchantress. At the same time, you bring a great risk with the blessing—so you have to be careful—Do you understand?"

James nodded looking unsure about what is happening, and Professor Galdor showed a paper that he had been holding in his hand giving it to James saying "I believe this belongs to you—you must learn and master your powers to be a fine enchanter like your mother. If not being involved without knowing your powers well is a great risk." said Professor Galdor looking closely at him.

Professor Galdor stood up pushing back his rich white cloak off the bed and walked towards the door with the pixie spirits in the hospital bowing in respect as he passed them.

James opened the letter and it looks like incomplete pieces of letters or symbols that were not understandable to the least bit. Suddenly in his mind, he could understand what was written as if he was fluent with the language so well. He reads the letter whispering so that no one around could hear him.

"dgatrone lefis deisto drege steees

dtrago deeske dist degastre

dedstra daine firdrats detes

daps dio den Burton"

He looked frightened and confused about what it tried to say, and he decided to translate it to English so that he could understand more clearly as he whispered the words to himself softly as he did before.

"The dusk awakes and goes to rest,

The darkness beams the powers of the hidden chest,

Two days more to save from his darkest best,

Burton's darkness awaits."

James felt a strong sense of danger to the Phrontistery and even the entire Pinnacle of Aries. He jumped out of the bed running towards the door as the spirit pixies looking shocked and one of them calling out saying "Boy stop—you cannot leave until noon!"

He runs out of the hospital through the hallway with walls that has shadows of flocks of birds flying all over the walls catching up to Professor Galdor.

"Sir wait!" James shouts as he runs up to him at the end of the hallway before enters his office.

Professor Galdor stops walking hearing James and turned around looking at James running towards him in complete surprise.

"James—what are you doing out of the hospital?"

"Sir I need—I need—I—" James was panting trying to catch some breath after running to catch the faculty president.

"Good heavens boy! Calm down—tell me what you want to say?" said Professor Galdor with a deeply concerned voice.

James finally was able to relax after a few deep breaths saying "Sir I am not sure how accurate this is— but I feel that we are in great danger. I need your help, sir."

Father Tolmen was walking down the hallway towards them with two heavy books in his hands, as he walks slowly listening to the disturbing conversation between James and the faculty president. He does not want to make it obvious that he has any interest in their conversation and therefore simply eavesdropping as he ambles down the hallway.

"What are you talking about James?" asked Professor Galdor narrowing the tough-looking wrinkled eyes.

"It is something to do about someone called Burton!" said James worriedly.

Father Tolmen takes his steps even slower and barely moving once he hears the name looking at Professor Galdor shocked. Professor Galdor notices father Tolemen's interest in the conversation and opens the door to his office.

"Come in James—Let's talk about this in private!" with his deep calm voice as he takes a quick look at father Tolmen before leading James into his office.

The walls in his office are filled with racks of paper bundles tied with a root string, books, a huge box named "pending approvals" on the side, and a classic typewriter on the table. He sits in his high back chair that's made with tree roots and cushioned with red feathers that shows a chair of high status and majestic. There was a big wooden table and three chairs for the visitors.

"Have a seat James!" said Professor Galdor looking at him while he puts on his glasses.

James sits down and looks up at Professor Galdor with a curious face.

 "Sir please tell me about Burton—I heard it's forbidden to discuss within the faculty—who is he?—Why is it forbidden to mention about him? Asks James.

"The name Burton is not just a person—well not anymore. I assume you attended your first history lesson about the land of Aries?" He asked James looking at him over his glasses.

James nodded as he looks at Professor Galdor with great curiosity.

"Burton is one of the children picked by Aries that joined the dark witchcrafts with greediness for power, and jealousy. He used the power of dark witchcrafts to make him immortal. The two children picked by Aries were given two power stones at a very young age and one contains a teardrop of the spirit dragon. Burton improvised his powers and abilities with dark witchcrafts with the use of his power stone which did not have a tear of the Spirit Dragon." Explained Professor Galdor.

"Is there any link between my mother and her powers with Burton sir?"

"Twenty years ago Burton attacked the Phrontistery to destroy the place that teaches the source powers and the place of future enchanters and enchantresses—there was only one enchantress who was able to protect the land of Aries with her blessings of the spirit dragon. She was the only enchantress who was born with the blessings after many generations—and the one who was gifted with the powers of the spirit dragon after the enchanter chosen by Aries. This enchantress had powers that we're able to defeat Burton—and this great enchantress was no other than your beloved mother Joanna Spinner!"

James was shocked with eyes wide and looking completely astonished hearing the bravery of his mother and the history of Burton.

"If you were warned in some way about some danger—then there is a great reason to it." said Professor Galdor.

"But why is it forbidden for the students to speak or know about him, sir?"

"The less the students know the safer they will be-—the powers of witchcraft are powerful that they might be able to access the Phrontistery through a student's interest mind."

"What should I do next sir?" asked James confusedly in a soft unsure voice.

"Just follow what your heart tells you to do— the signs that are being shown to you and your blessings will protect you!" replied Professor Galdor in his deep calm voice looking at James with great confidence.

James stood up and walked up to the door and paused turning back to face Professor Galdor.

"Sir!"

Professor Galdor looked up at James and bowed his head to look over his glasses.

"The book in the library sir—the faculty publisher said there were no more books printed and just two for the faculty reference—one to the library and one for you!" James said looking at the faculty president with great curiosity and hope to find the missing two pages.

"Do you have the book now?" asked professor Galdor.

"Yes but it's at the quarters—wait," James said suddenly putting his hand into the side pocket of his robe.

"I have the library card, sir," James said showing his card to Professor Galdor.

"Let me have a look—I should have a copy somewhere! Going through the messy racks of papers and books. "Let's go check on the faculty reference cupboards!"

They walked out of his office to a little room with tall cupboards filled with books. There was a board hanging on the wall that says "No Students Allowed".

"Here it is!" Professor Galdor said calmly turning the book cover and handing over the book to James with a slight smile on his face. Professor Galdor did not know what James was looking for in the book.

James quickly turned the page and to his surprise, he sees the exact two pages were torn off the book. "Oh no—It's missing in this too!" James said shockingly looking up at Professor Galdor with disappointment.

"What is missing dear boy?"

"The two pages—it's torn the same way as in the library book."

James replied worriedly. Professor Galdor took the book at once and adjust his glasses, he reads the content and turns the page. Taking deep breathing fretting as he touches the torn pages and looks up at James saying "I'm afraid you are right James—I think I have to discuss this with the management of the faculty—but I am not going to mention anything about you for your safety. It seems like there is someone inside the faculty hiding the links avoiding us being aware of how the enemies can access."

James looked at Professor Galdor shocked and worried seeing Professor Galdor highly concerned and looking at him feeling the obviousness of danger.

James walks down the hallway to his quarters and as he takes a turn he crashing onto another student walking towards him. James was definitely to be blamed as he was walking thinking about the warning and recalling everything that Professor Galdor told him.

"Watch where you are going James!" said in an arrogant voice which was no other than Wilbert and his friends.

"Sorry, Wilbert—I didn't see you." Replied James calmly

"Oh you didn't see me or you never heard me didn't you?—what did I tell you James!—to not try to be some star here—what are you up to now anyway?"

Asked Wilbert looking at him with a suspicious look.

The head student of Gravel congress walked towards them saying "Oh James! How are you?" and sees Wilbert "What are you doing here Wilbert?—you are supposed at lecturers which started half an hour ago!" asked the head student looking at him with a curious look.

"Just asking how our friend is doing!" Wilbert replied sarcastically with an insincere smile which instantly disappeared as he passed James looking at him with envious eyes.

Chapter Five: A Battle to Introduce

It is another typical day of lecturers and the daily tasks or schedules to be engaged with as usual, but not exactly to the management of the Phrontistery, and of course, the only four students who were aware of any danger that worried the president of the faculty was James, Laura, Henry, and Mathew. Professor Galdor is seated at the head of the table with Professor Cuppins, Father Tolmen, Professor Sisko, Professor Lansford, and two people that head the post-graduate faculty is in a serious discussion at the faculty boardroom. There are windows of stained glass, wide stone made long boardroom with floating light drops in the ceiling that brightens up the room shining the crafted polished wood of the board room chairs which are cushioned with red feathers on the seating.

"There is not a second thought that we ought to take every precaution to protect the Phrontistery and its students—especially the undergraduate students." Said Professor Galdor looking around at his staff.

"The undergraduate is at much greater risks—they cannot be in contact with any dangerous powers or situation on their own!" said Professor Cuppins

"That's right! They should be secured—postgraduates can handle to a reasonable extent in terms of their protection— besides they are no longer children! Said the head of Post-graduate faculty.

"Sir may I ask how did you get to know about the danger to the faculty?" asked Father Tolmen curiously.

"Should it matter Father Tolmen! I have been here, as the faculty president for over forty years, and predicting a future threat is part of my duty for the safety of all students and staff."

Professor Galdor looked at Father Tolmen with a furious look.

"That's true—we have to work together to take every precaution on the safety of the Phrontistery—the biggest target is the students—the core of the existence of future source powers who will be the only threat to the witchcrafts." Said Professor Sisko in his suave and calm voice.

"Inform the forces—tighten the security of the Phrontistery." Professor Galdor said in a tough stern voice.

"Yes sir!" replied Professor Cuppins with the head of post-graduate faculty nodding to accept the instructions.

It's the lunch hour and the faculty management seems in a rush with their issue at hand. It is only however noticeable to James, Laura, and the Davis brothers.

"I highly doubt Father Tolmen would keep it to himself if he had heard about speaking about the warning to Professor Galdor," said Laura.

Henry nodded saying "I agree—definitely would utter a word at least to Professor Cuppins."

"I don't think so!" Said James lost in deep thought.

"What are you thinking James?" asked Laura as they were walking back to their classes.

"I wonder if there is anything Father Tolmen knows that no one else knows." Replied James,

"James Look!" cried out Henry pointing at something out of the window.

"It's Darwin—He is sneaking into the woods just like he did the other day."

"Let's go!" said James running to see what Darwin is up to.

Darwin runs into the woods looking back being cautious as he runs and stops waiting for something. James, Laura, Mathew, and Henry hiding crouching behind a bush and curiously watching what Darwin is up to sneaking into the woods.

A skinny tall figure walked towards Darwin wearing a black robe with a trail that brushes the dried leaves on the ground, covering his head with a black hood and cloak. Darwin was speaking to the mysterious figure with great respect.

"Who is Darwin speaking to?" whispered Laura.

"It's difficult to see his face!"

Mathew peeping to have a look at the face and lost his balance by leaning forward a bit too much falling into the bush. The leaves and branches of the bush moved to make a light sound that gained the attention of Darwin and the mysterious figure.

"Oh no! Did they see us?" whispered Laura seeing Darwin walking towards the bush they were hiding. The mysterious figure was facing but impossible to see even with a slight raise of the heads, which will surely make them visible. James picked a stone and threw it in another direction making another slight sound that took Darwin's attention. He ran after it wanting to see what made the sound.

"Let's get out of here," said Henry about to leave with great fear.

"No! That person must be still on the watch—if we leave now whoever it is will see us." Mathew whispered holding his brother.

Darwin returned to the person and all of a sudden the mysterious person kicked Darwin that made him fall a few steps away as the tall figure shouted with rage in a raspy voice.

"You ineffectual worthless creature! I should have known you cannot do anything right!"

"Please my lord! I promise it will not happen again." Darwin pleaded in its humble voice as it tries to get on his feet holding his stomach seeming to be in pain of the strong kick.

"Poor Darwin!" said Henry looking at the helpless little elf.

The mysterious figure left walking into the woods but it was just instantly gone and nowhere to be seen, and Darwin ran away in another direction.

"Let's get out of here!" said James as they all stood up running out of the woods and emerged through the flower bushes that separates the land belonging to the Phrontistery.

The sound of the bells for their lecture sessions rings and it was the perfect timing. They all take a step forward away from the bushes and it is Professor Lansford. He looks at everyone with great curiosity and is displeased looking mostly at James.

"What is your business in the woods Spinner?"

"Nothing sir—we were just practicing the Gravel skills with trees and things—not too far Professor." Said Laura.

"Then what about these two in Adams Ale's doing in the forest?" Professor Lansford asked looking head to toe at the Davis brothers.

"We wanted to watch sir!" Henry responded with his face full of fear and swallowing a lump in his throat.

"You are not supposed to leave from the premises of the Phrontistery and out of these bushes without supervision of your teachers."

"Sorry Professor Lansford—it won't happen again." Mathew apologized.

He frowned looking unconvinced and walked away.

There were more spirit pixie guards like the two at the entrance of the Phrontistery building around the faculty fences and one at the entrances and in each hallway.

"Seems like the faculty is highly guarded than usual." Said Laura as they passed the guard who was standing at the entrance of their quarters.

"Why don't we ask Father Tolmen about the two missing pages of the book?" suggested Henry before they depart to go to their respective congress quarters.

"No!" James cried out.

"We sneak into the Father Tolmen's chamber tomorrow." Said James softly making sure no one around them could hear.

"What?" Laura squeaked surprised with James's plans.

"Shhh—let's talk about it tomorrow," whispered James seeing more students walking towards the quarters including Wilbert.

It was a usual Saturday morning and students are mostly at the library, quarters or at the study rooms.

"When Father Tolmen goes to his morning spirit guiding sessions we sneak into his chamber." Said James as he was walking down the hallway with Laura, Mathew, and Henry.

"Wait—there he is!" showed Mathew pushing Henry backward to cover behind the wall indicating to hide before Father Tolmen sees them.

Father Tolmen closes the door to his chamber with the usual pleasant face, and no way could he be involved in anything bad with his positive vibe and calmness he gives across the room.

"Let's go" whispered Mathew

They sneak out of the hallway and towards his chamber doors turning the gold doorknob slowly and entered into the simple bedroom on the side. A wall was full of books facing the bed with a messy table and a simple wooden chair facing the window.

They all started searching for the missing pages inside the chest of drawers, table, bookshelves, and any place they could think of the torn pages were hidden.

"Where is it!" said Laura giving up the search.

There was an opened envelop on the table that says "As you requested sire" and a folded letter inside the envelope. James took the paper inside unfolding it and looked at it with great shock and trembling fingers. The letter is a copy of an original death certificate.

"CERTIFICATE OF DEATH"

"This is to acknowledge the death of

"Joanna Shirley Spinner"

"AT: Wimbly   Hills Residencies"

"Cause of death: Cancer"

"What is it James?" asked Laura curiously.

"It's my mother's death certificate—and the one which is untrue!"

"What?—wonder what Father's Tolmen's business with it!" asked Mathew

"It could be for school reference and student personal records," said Henry calming down the tension in the room.

"But what is the request? Who had sent this to Father Tolmen?" asked Laura in deep thought.

"Wait—no one we could think of addresses saying sire—except…" Mathew uttered and suddenly looking up at James.

"Darwin!" said all four together.

"What are we going to do James?" asked Laura looking at the paper in his hand.

"We go talk to Darwin one on one!" James replied courageously.

"James—Wait—that's too dangerous, and we can't ask him directly!" said Henry.

"Yes, I can! This information belongs to my mother and I have the most right to know why Father Tolmen has any interest in my mother's death." James replied with a dominant voice.

They walked towards the elves' quarters that were on the other side of the faculty building surrounded by a wooden fence. There was a row of tiny houses made with dark stone walls and wooden roofs. An elf lady wearing a ragged gown with a blue scarf covering her head is harvesting lettuce in the garden.

"Excuse me miss!' shouted Laura.

The elf looked up holding the palm basket filled with lettuce in one hand.

"Do you know where Darwin is?—the helper elf at the faculty?" asked Henry.

The elf woman pointed in a direction showing Darwin who was stacking wood at a distance.

"Thank you!" said Henry to the elf as she bowed in respect with a smile.

"Darwin!" James called out as he turned around stacking the wood right on top of the pile smiling as if he is happy to see James.

"Oh sire—it's lovely to see you—not many come to visit me," Said Darwin.

"We need to ask you something!" said Laura.

"Certainly Dame—I am always at your service!"

"What is this?" James asked showing Darwin the copy of the death certificate.

"Oh—I don't know sire" replied Darwin with fear and looking around panicking.

"Of course you know Darwin—you sent this to Father Tolmen didn't you?" asked Henry taking a step forward when Darwin take a step back. It was obvious with Darwin's reaction that he knew something about it. James, Laura, Mathew, and Henry all looking at Darwin ireful waiting for Darwin's response.

"Oh, sire—there is nothing this elf of two penny–half penny could do. I am only doing what I am asked to do under the thrall of my masters."

Liar! Exclaimed James.

"What is going on here?—James?" Professor Galdor asked walking towards them.

Darwin took the chance and ran away while Professor Galdor approach James, Laura, and the David brothers.

"Sir—I" James tried to explain stammering with fear since they stole the information from Father Tolmen's chambers.

"Let's talk about it later—The Phrontistery is under attack—some students are attacked at the Rose Dale corridors—to your quarters—now!" demanded Professor Galdor.

Laura, James, and Davis brothers all ran into the faculty building through an alternative entrance door that leads up the stairs and into the Spring Valley corridors of the faculty. They turned to another hallway and passing a female student fainted on the floor.

"I think I'm going to faint too" uttered Henry with fear.

"What has he done to those students on the floor?" asked James while running to their quarters.

"That's an attack for a warning—it's a spell by the witches to be unconscious for about ten hours." Said Laura.

"This way!" said Mathew and running in another direction of the hallway. The shortcut Mathew showed led them to the hallway that leads to their quarter doors.

The knight spirit pixies were attacked and disappeared turning into sand with their spears and shields fallen all over the floor. The mysterious figure that James, Laura, and the brothers saw in the woods after following Darwin was standing right at the end of the hallway staring at them through the black hood with a face unseen.

Professor Lansford and Professor Galdor came running and stood right behind him full of fear and surprise. Professor Lansford stretched his arms and brought his hand together pointing his fingers at the hooded man. Two soldiers emerged with swords and shields from the walls of Welkins that flows on the walls beside them. The water spirit soldiers stabbed the hooded man making him scream with pain turning into a cloud of black smoke and disappeared along with his loud echoing howl.

"To your quarters now!" shouted Professor Galdor.

James, Laura, Henry, and Mathew ran towards the quarters jumping over the dead spirit pixie knights and to the congress quarter doors. Laura and James ran into the Gravel doors and the David brothers into the welkins. There was a row of climber plants with flowers right in front, and before the first two beds of the dorm securing from anyone entering any further. A row of tall green plant stems with upper bodies of green soldiers wearing green helmets with a comb, visor, helm, and a fully covered medieval war soldier kit made with brown rocks covering the necks, arms, and chest till above the waistline holding swords. The climber parts moved to clear the path for Laura and James to walk in and join the rest of the students all standing at the back of the boy's quarters and mostly in the girl's quarters of the Gravel congress. There were two post-graduate students, both in the early twenties wearing green cloaks and power stones controlling the row of climber plant soldiers.

"Thank goodness you both are safe—go on now!" said one of the young men assuring James and Laura are now safe.

James and Laura walked into the quarters feeling lost and worried at the same time.

"This is not right—we've got to do something!"

"But James it's too dangerous, and we are still not aware the right way to fight Burton. At least not yet!" said Laura concernedly.

"Please show me the way!" James whispered to himself hoping his powers with the spirit dragon will guide him. Just as he requested he heard the rattle sound and walked towards the soldier spirits guarding before the congress quarter door.

"Stop—where do you think you are going? Shouted one of the young men holding a power stone.

Strangely the soldier plants moved to bow their heads allowing James to walk through and out of the doors with respect.

"We got to try harder—Professor Galdor will not be pleased if we let him out!" said one of the post-graduate students to the other.

"I am trying—the spirit soldiers moves against our control."

James walked out of the doors and walks out through the hallways following the rattle sound and running down the main staircase passing the water fountain with the rattle getting louder and louder. He sees the little spirit pixie fairy in the water fountain that's usually happy, friendly, and bubbly cowed and hiding between bushes shivering in fear.

"It's going to be alright—I promise," James said calmly and she raised her head slightly smiling at him feeling secure.

James was lead to the entrance door of the faculty and out of the building guided by the rattle. He saw the mysterious hooded man floating in the air staring at him much taller than the human size he saw in the hallway.

"I was expecting you, James," the hooded man said in his husky voice. It is dark with nightfall and unusually windy. The black cloak of the hooded man was moving and waving behind him against the wind.

"I know who you are—I am not afraid of you!" shouted James with rage.

"Hmm—courageous and stubborn at its best—just like your mother aren't you?"

"Don't you dare speak about my mother Burton—you are a murderer"

"Oh you are wise—you do know my name—but—I didn't kill your mother James—she killed herself"

"No!" James exclaimed.

 James used his powers stretching the branch of the trees that surrounds the Phrontistery wrapping Burton's body and trying to crush his flesh and bones. A high source of power used by Burton struck lightning to the ground around the Phrontistery exploding the branches wrapped around him into pieces without any effort. The lightning was loud with a heavy vibration and a force that's so strong attacking James and throwing him backward hitting him on the entrance doors and falling hard on the wooden floor.

"This is quite an introduction James— I was longing to meet you in person!" said Burton in a sarcastic husky voice.

"Leave the boy alone!" shouted Professor Cuppins as she rushed out of the entrance along with Professor Galdor and the rest of the lecture panel including Father Tolmen. Professor Sisko helped James to get up, while the professors were standing near the steps at the entrance of the Phrontistery looking at Burton with great worry and fear.

"Do you know the problem with the discipline in your faculty?" asked Burton sarcastically.

"None of you have the slightest idea of how to be a good host to your guest!"

Professor Sisko used his powers belonging to Adam's Ale creating water knights that look half-human wearing helmets and body armor to prepare for war with tails of sea horses holding bows and arrows aiming at Burton. When the arrows were released Burton used his powers and attacks back with strong thunder strikes against the water knights evaporating all of them into thin air. Professor Sisko did not want to give up and made another set of water knights, and Professor Galdor attacks covering Burton into a tornado with his source powers as a Welkin, yet Burton stands strong inside the tornado swirl. Professor Lansford uses his powers of an enchanter of Gravel growing strings of roots from the ground towards Burton tying his hands and neck holding him in place to stop him from moving or use his hands to attack back. Seeing Burton being attacked with the three source powers by three mighty enchanters who have mastered skills and knowledge so well made Burton powerless only for just short as few seconds. There was a sudden force with a wave of fire thrown burning the roots into ashes, and combining the fire with the tornado turning from an air to a bright fire tornado moving to the water knights evaporating just as it did before. The fire tornado burst with a strong wind and a vibration that was traveling towards the Phrontistery.

"Everyone get down!" shouted Professor Galdor as he gets down on the floor along with the rest of the lecturers, and Professor Cuppins holding James lying down covering him on the wooden floor.
The vibration wave traveled above their heads and across the Phrontistery building making the strong stone-built walls, the strong wooden floors, and ceilings slightly quiver. The vibration wave passed and disappeared, as the dust between the roots of the ceilings fall with flower drops fallen everywhere without its bright yellow glow. The lecturers and James slowly stood up as the surrounding are now calm and quiet and Burton stands on the ground size back to an average human walking towards them. James closed his eyes and opened not with his usual dark eyes, but eyes of a pigeon bright orange and yellow with a dark black pupil looking directly at Burton. Professor Galdor looked at James and he knew it was no in their hands and the power of the spirit dragon is now a presence. He asked the rest of the lecturers to stand back allowing James to take over with his authentic powers of the spirit dragon. Burton attacked directly at them striking thunders as he walked faster towards them. James stretched his arms forward building a wall of bright red flames that blocked the thunder strikes and pushed the red flamed wall towards Burton making him disappear with a painful howl. Burton was no longer at sight and the lecturers looking around to make sure if he is gone. James' eyes were back to his own as he looked around him worryingly. Despite the physical presence of Burton is no longer there the husky voice spoke from nowhere.

"I am impressed with your fearlessness and courage James—let's consider this battle as the one that introduced ourselves and to a new beginning—we shall meet again!"

The voice disappeared and the presence of Burton at the Phrontistery is now gone but with the threat that the battle just began.

"James are you alright?" asked Professor Galdor.

"Yes sir!"

"Let's get you into your quarters," said Professor Cuppins taking James back into the Phrontistery.

They went into the faculty and it was not the neatly kept interior but messy and wrecked with the vibration that went through the faculty. There were some light drops fallen without its glow, chairs and some furniture toppled and fallen, papers and books all over the ground with the well-polished wooden floors now dusty with the dust on the ceilings fallen between the roots. The flowers on the walls of the Gravel congress look slightly wilted with spirit pixie knights that were guarding in every hallway and corner of the faculty killed and dropped dead on the floors. The lecturers and James walked through the hallways and up the main stairways to go to the congress quarters. The little spirit pixie fairy quickly flying out of the bushes and watching the lecturers and James walking upstairs in great wonder.

Professor Cuppins, James and Professor Galdor went into the Gravel quarter doors with the post-graduate students, and used the powers to make the climber plant soldiers vanish to walk into the quarters. The students seated on the floors and beds all stood up looking at James and the Professor in surprise and confused not knowing what was going on out of the quarter doors.

"Everything is fine students—take some rest and we shall meet you at the dining rooms for breakfast—you do not have the morning sessions tomorrow due to restoring processes in the faculty." Said Professor Cuppins calmly.

"Also there is no need to get up all lazy and grumpy tomorrow since we decided to give you an extra hour of sleep—therefore breakfast will be served at eight thirty and after tomorrow you will be back with your usual schedules," said Professor Galdor in a bit of jolly voice and for a tranquil environment.

"We should go to the other congress quarters sir—let's check if everyone is alright," said Professor Cuppins.

"Certainly Professor Cuppins!"

The two professors left with the two post-graduate students joining them.

"James—are you alright?" asked Laura walking up to him.

"Yes

"Let's go meet Mathew and Henry," said Laura as they both went out of the Gravel quarters.

James and Laura walked towards the Adam's Ale congress quarters and the Davis brothers met them on the way.

"We were about to come to the Gravel to check if you both are okay!"

"Yes we are fine—are you two okay?" asked Laura

"Yes we are fine too" responded Mathew calmly.

"What happened out there, James? Asked Laura curiously while Mathew and Henry looked at James waiting for his response.

"Burton is too powerful and he uses the powers of the spirit dragon with his power stone." Said, James.

"Did you fight him?" asked Mathew.

"Yes, and the professors—he did go away but said he will come back—we should do something to find a way to make him powerless."

"There should be a way with your born powers of the spirit dragon—that's the only source power that's strong enough to fight his," said Laura.

"By the way—should we tell about Darwin to Professor Galdor?" asked Henry inquisitively,

"No—I feel it's too soon," said James

"James is right! If we keep an eye on Darwin and figure out what he is really up to—it will help us to find a lot of things," said Mathew

Laura nodded in agreement saying "That's true! Besides we don't have enough proof to tell anything about Darwin yet—apart from the fact that we saw Darwin speaking to Burton in the woods."

"Well—the only way we can say it is Burton is because the person he was speaking to was wearing a black long robe and a black cloak with a hood. That's not an unusual attire around here at Aries, and he could say it was anyone else too. Said Henry.

"But I do think our best clue is Darwin—we must know why he sent your mother's false death certificate to father Tolmen" Said Mathew.

"I am still not clear about one thing —you said that the students were fainted as a result of the attack for about ten hours as a warning?" asked Henry looking confused at Laura.

"Yes I did"

"How do you know precisely they were just fainted?" asked Henry with James and Mathew looking at Laura curiously waiting for an answer.

"There is no reason for Burton to take the consciousness of a student who doesn't have his or her power stone."

They were all still confused yet when James was about to ask something after Laura's response the bells rang, and the students ran back to their quarters hurrying than usual. It surely was a night to everyone that disturbs, worries and fear all at the Phrontistery very much.

Chapter Six: Another Attack

The morning arises after a long day and an extra hour of sleep is treasure especially for James. He was exhausted and woke up with body pains with the strong hit on the entrance doors. He sat on his bed and the boy next to him slightly snoring with his mouth open not a disturbing yesterday can affect any change for his love for sleeping. James was sitting on the bed thinking about everything he experienced last night. A group of senior students walked in with the sound of the quarter doors of Gravel slammed and nearly tearing off the hinges. It is Wilbert with his friends walking towards James looking furious and almost to explode taking the attention of all the boys around the male quarters, and of course the ones only awake.

"James!" shouted Wilbert waking up the boy sleeping next to him.

"Hey—could you be quiet and let me sleep?' the boy said scratching his drowsy eyes.

"Shut up!" shouted Wilbert making the boy helplessly quiet with fear.

"What is it now Wilbert? Asked James calmly.

Wilbert gave a lop-sided grin turning to his friends as they all laughed at James, but seemingly they laughed because Wilbert wanted them to and save their selves without any trouble from their so-called leader of that friend group.

He grabbed from James's collars of his pajama shirt looking with rage and about to punch him on the face.

"What did I tell you, James?—didn't I tell you not to be a star around here! You have stepped out of line Spinner—who do you think you are anyway!"

"The savior of the Phrontistery," said a familiar deep male voice at the back.

They all turned around to see who and Wilbert with his stormy temper, and it was Professor Galdor walking towards frowning at the senior students. Wilbert's anger disappeared and changed to fear as he looks at the faculty president looking utterly displeased.

"What are you boys doing here?" asked Professor Galdor calmly.

"Professor Galdor—we were just—um—we came to see how James is doing—and" stammering for a great excuse for their presence.

"That's a funny way to see if someone's well." Said professor Galdor sarcastically and shouted at the senior students and especially looking directly at Wilbert saying "Leave now!"

Wilbert and his friends rushed passing Professor Galdor and left the Gravel quarter doors.

"How are you James?" asked Professor Galdor looking at James calmly

"I am fine sir—thank you!"

"We are very proud of your bravery James—you will be a fine enchanter one day!" said Professor Galdor calmly, and smiled at James.

The building was mostly repaired with new light drops and two elves wearing maid costumes were sweeping the dining room. There were plant specialists in the Gravel congress curing the wilted climber plants and little maid elves sweeping and cleaning the broken glass pieces, fallen light drops, and arranging the new furniture. James, Laura, and the Davis brothers were all at the breakfast table. Professor Galdor and the rest of the lecture panel walked into the dining room and the entire room was silenced and settled. All the lecturers were seated except Professor Galdor who was announcing with great sorrow.

"Good morning students! We apologize for what you all had to face last night—and it was an unforgettable night for all of us. We thank you for your corporation and courage—and thank you for being in your best discipline adhering to the rules of the Phrontistery. We lost three students and —we have organized a special service at the Forest Lake Chapel tomorrow four in the evening and we expect all of your presence. Also, we lost twenty-eight of our spirit pixie knights sacrificing their lives and their service can never be forgotten. I also want to say on behalf of the Phrontistery we will do everything under our power to keep you safe—we have tightened some rules of the faculty for your safety and we hope all of you will obey them as you are expected."

Some students were greatly saddened and probably seem like close friends of the three students who couldn't make it through the awful night. The rest of the students still disturbed and worried whispering to each other, and the surrounding was not like any other day but with the absence of a relaxed environment. The table runners were black soft feathers and the walls of Gravel blooms only with flowers that change an off-white to a bright white texture apart from the dark beautifully textured flowers. Professor Cuppins stood

up upset and seems a bit exhausted than usual announcing

"The rules have being taken a step further towards the safety of the students of the Phrontistery—student has

to be in your quarters by eight post-dinner and not allowed to be roaming around apart from the classrooms

during your lecture schedules and the areas you are supposed to be such as the library, dining room, study

rooms and any other places you should under a supervision of a lecturer.—Let us be in a moment of silence

for our three beloved students and the spirit knights who lost their lives as a result of the tragic night."

All the students were up and bowing their heads while James heard a cry of a woman who was loud and

sobbing. He looked up and it was a spirit pixie in their table in front wearing a long white gown made of a

long and wide water-lily bud and hair that was a flow of water.

"Who is that?" James asked whispering to Laura

"That's the Queen of Lotus—Esther—she is a mermaid and a protector of the lotus dynasty in the lake. She

is a real beauty conscious and combs her hair for hours sitting on a rock beside the lake.

"But that's water!" said James fully confused.

"Well—for her it's not!" Laura replied.

She starting to cry louder weeping for the night and the loss of the knights and on behalf of the students

despite if she knows any of them personally. The cry was too loud to bear and a sharp screech.

"She gets a little too sensitive sometimes," said Laura sarcastically, and the loud weep surely makes Wilbert

gall as he slams a napkin on the table frowning at the emotional spirit pixie.

James, Mathew, Laura, and Henry are all at the library studying till the lecturers are back as in the schedules.

Almost all the students are either at the library or the study room mostly chatting away and much relaxed

than being completely focused, unlike the classrooms. The old elf librarian lady is hushing and scowling at

the students to maintain the best noiseless environment. There was a slight loud giggle within a bunch of

girls at a corner table.

"Shhh—this isn't your quarters" whispered the lady frowning as she looks over her large round glasses.

Laura, James, and the Davis brother seated on the feather carpet floor between two shelves studying with their textbooks.

"We got to find Darwin," said James whispering to the others.

"I think this is the best time to do that—let's check in the lobby area," said Mathew

The four stood up and left the library to look for Darwin walking through the hallways towards the lobby.

On the way to the lobby Father Tolmen was walking towards them looking calm with a pleasant smile.

"I was waiting to speak to you James—thank you for your bravery last night—we could have faced a greater damage if it wasn't for you."

"It was an honor to fight on behalf of the Phrontistery father!" replied James.

"I shall see you all in class!" Said Father Tolmen as walked away smiling in the calmest and friendly manner.

"Darwin is nowhere—maybe he is still home," said Laura.

They walked to the little elf quarters at the faculty passing the row of little houses, and an elf stacking wood was sighted as they all walked towards him.

"Excuse me—do you know where Darwin is? We need to speak to him!"

"He is missing since yesterday noon!" said the old elf man.

"Yesterday noon!'' Mathew looked at James in utter surprise.

 Let's go back—I don't want to get ourselves in trouble being in a place we shouldn't be!" said Henry.

As they walked back in the middle of the corridor was a red feather a bit longer than of an ordinary pigeon.

James picked up the feather and as they walked further turning to a hallway that had the music class, there was another feather fallen on the ground near the staircase. The staircase at the end of the hallway leads to the bell tower of the faculty.

"C'mon!" said James asking everyone to follow him running towards the stairs.

The bell tower was narrow and long with two long rows of gold-plated heavy metal bells. There was someone on the other end of the room, but the room was a bit too dark to see who. The octagon-shaped window at the back gave a beam of light to the back of the figure. It was visible that a person is a man with a bald head.

"Father Tolmen—is that you?" asked Mathew looking curiously at the figure.

"Who are you?" asked James.

"I am very much disappointed that you don't recognize who I am!" said the man, and he sounds exactly like Father Tolmen.

"Father Tolmen—you just spoke to us in the hallway a few minutes ago—what are you doing here?" asked Mathew as he walked towards him to see the man properly.

At once the man-made a strong wind as the bells rang not in the usual smooth melody but a one loud and out of tune to hear. They covered their ears from their palms as the noise was too loud and noisy, and James looked up at the man and he was approaching slowly towards them.

"Hello James!" said the man changing from the voice of father Tolmen to a husky voice that sounds exactly like Burton.

"What are you doing here? Asked James looking at him in great anger.

"Just came by to say hello!" said Burton as he walks in the middle of the two rows of metal bells.

Henry shivering in fear, and his face almost to cry and shouted saying "Let's get out of here!" and ran towards the crude wooden door.

It shut on its slamming right in front of Henry and the rest trapping inside the bell tower.

"Stop playing games Burton!" shouted James.

"I admire your courage James—you are just like your mother."

"You killed her!" shouted Laura with anger.

"I didn't kill her child—she wasn't very fond with sharing things—I only wanted to use her power stone but she overreacted."

"How dare you!" shouted James as he used his powers to grow a tree branch through the window breaking the glass to attack Burton.

"I see from where you get your habit of overreacting James!" said Burton and attacked Laura as she fell on the floor unconsciously.

"No—Laura!" cried out James as they all gathered and kneeling around her.

James looked around the darkroom but Burton has disappeared, and the branch was gone which was through the window only with a hole in the stained window glass.

The door opens and Professor Cuppins and Professor Sisko entered standing and staring at them with great shock.

"What are you all doing here?" asked Professor Cuppins displeased and quickly walked towards Laura as she crouched down on the floor placing her hand on Laura's chest feeling her heartbeat.

"I will inform the hospital," said Professor Sisko as he runs downstairs with his rich blue cloak sweeping the steps behind him.

A spirit pixie with a body and limbs made with long green climber plant stems and a leaf textured light greenish face walked in and picked up Laura as the thin stems wrapped around her knees and body while a slightly broad leaf held her head carefully to secure and carried her to the hospital.

"What happened here James?" asked Professor Sisko

"It was him—Burton," said James

There were students gathered around seeing the events of a student being carried by a hospital spirit pixie unconscious. Professor Galdor was seen rushing towards the bell towers looking worried, and walking through the student crowd as they moved aside giving him sufficient space.

James, Mathew, Henry, and the two professors came downstairs from the bell tower following the hospital spirit pixie carrying Laura.

"Another attack—professor Cuppins please arrange a staff meeting—immediately." commanded Professor Galdor.

"Yes sir!"

"We need to secure the faculty—inform the forces and get some knights to guard the faculty." Said Professor Galdor exhausted and worried.

"With all respect sir—last time we had enough knights for an army to secure the Phrontistery, but some way or another it didn't stop from Burton entering the premises," said Professor Lansford frowning and slightly displeased as usual.

"That's true Professor Lansford!—but this time the target is not the Phrontistery but to one and one person only."

"I assume you mean—James—sir!" said Professor Cuppins.

Professor Galdor slowly nodded worriedly.

It wasn't like any ordinary day for Mathew, James, and Henry as they attended all their lectures and days schedule without Laura.

 It's the second day after the attack and Laura still lying on the hospital bed unconscious. James and the Davis brothers visits her morning and afternoon and while they were walking back to the congress quarters Professor Cuppins came walking towards them with great panic.

"James —I need to speak to you!"

She looked at them worriedly and held James's shoulder with a glance at the David brothers saying "She is missing—the faculty searched everywhere but she is nowhere in the faculty or the hospital. We still got search parties—we are doing everything we can to find her."

"Missing!" said Henry worried looking at his brother, James, and lastly at Professor Cuppins.

James, Henry, and Mathew rushed to the hospital looking closely at the bed she was lying on. There was a bare footprint on the wooden floor right next to the bed.

"Look!" pointed Mathew at the muddy footprint on the floor.

"Seems like an adult's footprint—who walked from outdoors without shoes!" said James curiously crouching down and looking at the footprint on the floor.

"It's mud—it could be from the forest!"

They walked out of the hospital and walked into the woods looking around for a clue. There was a bare footprint on the ground that matches the footprint they saw on the hospital floor.

"Look!" said James

"It's Darwin—what is he doing here?"

"Darwin!" shouted James running towards the elf.

He ran away frightened seeing the boys into the deeper woods looking back seeing them running behind him. Darwin was caught by the back of the ragged shirt by James and held him down turning him to face him holding him down on the ground.

"Speak Darwin—enough of your hide and seek! I know you know about Laura's disappearance."

"Please sire! It is not hidden and seeks" pleaded Darwin.

"Tell us where Laura is Darwin— whom you were speaking to in the woods the other day?" asked Mathew looking furious.

"Please sire—don't shout—He will kill me if he knows you followed me."

"He?" asked Henry frowning down at Darwin.

James held from Darwin's shoulders shaking him shouting with great rage and impatience saying "Tell us, Darwin—where is she? Did he take her? You know where Burton is don't you?"

Using all his strength Darwin struggled to get himself loose and ran away.

"Stop—Darwin" shouted Mathew as they ran behind him into the woods having to stop just at one point without any sight of Darwin.

They looked around and it was a space in the middle of the forest in a fine clear circle with tall oak trees covering the space. They looked around to see the circle of empty ground, and its surrounding looked the same covered with the tall oak trees with no sight of Darwin.

"Look!" showed Henry pointing towards the ground, and seeing something written on the soil that says "Sire I am here only to show the way, all you have to do is trust me. The hide is to find and to seek is by trust"

They saw Darwin peeping from a tree a few feet away looking at them, and expecting them to follow his lead. They kept running with Darwin appearing from a tree to another to find a diary on the ground. James picked up the wood-crafted diary that has engraved with the name Laura Wilson.

"This is Laura's Diary," said James confused and worried.

He turned the pages of the diary and to find the date she was attacked with just the date written in her handwriting 16th September 2008, and the next two pages till today's date written with different handwriting with the date "17th" on one page and "18th" on the other with the phrase same as on the ground saying "Hide is to find and seek is by trust."

"James this is a trap!" said Mathew looking around worried and confused.

"Why don't we take this to Professor Galdor?" said Henry with his usual face almost about to cry in fear in a point of trouble.

"Look its Laura!" shouted Mathew sighting her lying on the ground unconscious. They ran towards her and kneeled trying to wake her up.

"Laura wake up!"

"Err—Guys! What's that noise?" said Henry feared for life

They heard a slight roar in the background and a full black lion appeared as it approached with its steps with great might slowly towards them. It had the eyes of a reptile and not just an ordinary lion but the comparison of the most incomparable creature with eyes vicious-looking like its prey right in front of it. James, Mathew, and Henry stood up and pulled back Laura as they slowly stepped back as the lion steps forward.

As it got close it suddenly burst into a cloud of black smoke and disappeared. As they looked up it was Phanto the spirit pixie at the faculty holding a bow in his hand as he floats slightly above the ground.

"What are you doing here?" asked Phanto with his calm pleasant voice yet concerned.

"We found her! We got to get her to the hospital" replied James finally feeling relief.

Phanto carried Laura effortlessly and left the woods and to the hospital. "Oh, thanks to the heaven of Aries," said the hospital spirit pixie lady as she came running towards Phanto to take Laura.

"I will inform the faculty," said Phanto and left the hospital.

"What is wrong with her? She will be fine soon won't she?" asked Mathew from the spirit pixie. She looked at them full of disappointment and sympathy as she looked at Laura lying unconscious on the bed and her friends waiting to hear if she will recover soon.

Professor Galdor, Professor Cuppins, and Professor Sisko came rushing into the hospital looking shocked.

"Where did you find her?" asked Professor Cuppins clutching her chest with both hands.

"We found her in the woods!" replied Mathew

"You children went to the woods?" asked Professor Cuppins fully displeased.

"It is a great thing you boys found her—but you shouldn't leave without informing us—it is for your safety." Said Professor Galdor calmly

"Yes sir—we understand!" replied Mathew.

James and the Davis brothers were heading back to their congress quarters through the hallways of Gravel, and turning to the hallways with walls representing the powers of Adam's Ale with the beautiful calming waterfall flows with the wonders of the sources powers. They heard someone running behind them with bare feet as the flesh of the feet hit the wooden floor. They all quickly turned around only to find no one behind them.

"Did both of you hear someone just running towards us?" asked James confused.

"No doubt!" said Mathew looking at his brother with the face of fear about to cry as usual.

"Who just followed us?" asked Henry with a high-pitched trembling voice.

"Look" cried out James showing muddy footprints on the floor.

"Show yourself!" said James looking around the empty hallway.

"I said show yourself!"

"Uhhh" cried out James covering his ears and falling on the floor on his knees.

"James are you alright?" asked Henry holding James from his shoulder.

The rattle sound is heard loud inside James's ears and its volume unbearable that shuts the eyes tight and reduces gradually as he opens with his eyes of a pigeon and he ends up standing in a different ground, place, and a completely different world. A place surrounded by red mountains and ground with bright glowing sand. Trees with red, orange, light green leaves and a sky of a beautiful gradient of purple, orange, and magenta clouds in the dark blue sky.

"Welcome young enchanter! I have been waiting for you" said in a most smoothing yet majestic voice with an echo from the sky.

"Who are you?" asked James looking around confused.

Right then landed the most magical creature way larger than a mammoth with long dragon wings, neck, and face with bright red feathers and eyes resembles a pigeon's face. A mouth of a dragon with a red snout instead of a beak and with the most sparkling and half-closed pigeon eyes looking graciously at James. The beige scales with brownish rings on its tail so long that it's around its feet wrapped to a wide three-tier circle and on the top tier was the massive tip of its tail is a rattle in brown. It was nothing like a pigeon, dragon, or snake James had ever seen or could imagine. In its chest was a big round stone glowing in yellow light with bright red flames inside it.

"You are the spirit dragon!" said James looking completely amazed.

"James—I am with you to guide and protect you—but you must seek the truth and fight for what is right! You must not be trapped in your world of fears and any other that could get you weak" said the spirit dragon as each word echoing in the background.

"I am not scared or weak—it's just that everything is unclear and I feel lost."

A woman wearing a long white robe walked from afar towards James smiling kindly, and her face looking so familiar and recognizable.

"Mom!"

"My son—it's so lovely to see you again"

"Mother, what happened to you? Why you had to leave?"

"I never wished to leave son—at least not that soon—but I am here because my powers were taken. But if you come with me I can come back to you."

The woman reached out her hand for James to join her.

"Yes mother—I will," said James and ran towards her and held her hand in an instant. As soon as he held her hand she changed to a statue of glowing sand and collapsed on the floor."

"No mom—where are you?" Shouted James and looking at the spirit dragon full of tears.

"Please bring her back!" James pleaded

"James—your emotions will make you weak—so weak it may take you to things different to what is real— fall for the illusions and traps of the evil."

"But my mother…" He looked where his mother was standing but there is no sign that a person was standing there which was only just unreal.

"James—to be strong you need to accept the reality and then you will be able to see what is hidden—and the answer for what is hidden in the trust to see it."

"Was it you who took Laura as a test master?"

"Laura was taken by the evil to lead you to them—all I did is guide you and bringing your dear friend back to you—that does not mean the evil is defeated—you still have a much bigger purpose."

"But there was a footprint on the floor next to the bed—the same footprint I saw in the hallway before I came here!" Said James curiously

"You will not be here if you didn't follow my sign—and to give your friend back—she is here physically but her mind and consciousness is still with Burton"

"Is there any way I can bring her conscious back master?"

The spirit dragon flew away flapping its massive wings in the air saying "Accept the reality—answer the hidden with trust."

James opened his eyes and he was kneeling in the middle of the hallway they were walking, and the two brothers looking at James utterly confused.

"James—James—say something—what happened to you?"

"I met the spirit dragon," said James with eyes wide.

"You what?" said the Davis brothers together full of disbelief.

"Accept the reality—answer the hidden with trust," said James softly looking down and lost in deep thought.

He stood up and walked passing Henry and Mathew towards the congress quarters leaving the Davis brothers in confusion and their jaws dropped.

"I think he's losing it!" said Henry walking behind James to their quarters with his brother.

Chapter Seven: Family Comes First

James had no sleep thinking and recalling the moment of meeting of the spirit dragon and the image of his

mother even though it's just an illusion. The bells rang to start the day and James hopped out of bed, got

ready, and grabbed the books running out of the quarter doors wanting to meet Mathew and Henry.

"Good morning James," said Henry as he walked up to James with Mathew.

"Good morning! We got speak to Phanto—He might know something about the cave behind the waterfall."

"But shouldn't we find a way to cure Laura before anything else?" asked Mathew stopping James as they

were walking towards the hallway.

"That's exactly what we are going to do—now c'mon!" said James running towards the hallways of the

classrooms where Phanto can be usually found.

Phanto was speaking to two boys seemingly a friendly conversation with Phanto's personality to get along

with the teachers, students, and other spirit pixies.

"Phanto!" cried out James as they ran towards Phanto.

"Hello James—is everything alright?"

"Yes—but we want to ask you something important!"

"What is it?"

 "Do you know anything about the cave in the woods?" asked James

"The one behind the waterfall?" asked Mathew

Phanto looked around worriedly and looked at James and the Davis brothers saying "Come with me!"

They walked to a corner to find some privacy and where no one could do any eavesdropping or having to

hear accidentally

"The cave was an old house of a spirit pixie—the house of the Spirit of the mortal."

"The spirit who married the first enchanter!" said Mathew surprised.

"That's right—the spirit was killed by Burton. She gave birth to two children—the son was born with the

spirit dragon's blessings, and the other was a daughter— a talented enchantress herself. Both married to the human world, but the children of the generations were born as enchanters and enchantresses while a very few did not. We believe the spirit of mortal was killed by Burton for greediness to power, and the house was cursed and everything of the Spirit of Mortal including her story was hidden in history in the Phrontistery even her belongings—like her house."

"But why?" asked James curiously.

"Burton used his cunning mind and understood the only way to trap your mother is through illusion of your father. He found out who your father was—and so he killed him, and created illusions bringing your mother to the trap which was the house that belonged to the spirit of Mortal. The spirit dragon helped your mother to escape and she was a new post-graduate who got her power stone a few days ago. That was the first time she discovered a true born blessings of the spirit dragon, and experiencing the true powers of the Spirit Dragon. Her power stone is like no other—the most powerful by-born blessings of the spirit dragon. Your mother was saved by the spirit dragon and her talent to defeat Burton was her own skills of Gravel source powers. Burton was more powerful and succeeded in taking her power stone. It's from your mother's power stone Burton is able to do what he did to Laura. The house was used by the witchcrafts as the prison to kidnap spirit pixies to use them as slaves with their conscious being controlled and to practice dark magic. The place was protected with a curse of the witchcrafts—but your mother and the faculty management defeated Burton and the tribe with the help of the spirit dragon, and freed the spirit pixies including me by removing the curse. The Phrontistery hid the history for the safety of the students and the cave with a waterfall build by the powers of Adam's Ale to keep the students out of the forest and within the Phrontistery premises." Phanto explained in his calming and pleasant voice.

"What about the power stone?" Henry asked with great curiosity.

"Actually Mrs. Spinner gave her power stone to Burton."

"But why?" asked James surprised and frowning his eyebrows.

"The reason—is still unknown! It made her powerless to protect herself and she was murdered by Burton."

"But how did I end up in the human world?" asked James.

"After your mother found out she was going to have a child she went to the human world to be away from Burton. Your mother's murder and your true identity was hidden to you by your family with the intention of staying away from Burton." Said Phanto looking at James with great sympathy.

"But why was everything hidden to her own nephew?" asked Henry angry with the injustice to his friend.

"To keep her sister's son away—away from finding out the truth, and to avoid him from being the next powerful enchanter with born blessings of the spirit dragon. Phanto explained as he turned to James. Once we knew you were ready and the right age—the faculty management got you here."

James looked at Phanto shocked but emotionally moved at the same time. Phanto touched James's shoulder looking at his eyes with great confidence.

"You are here for a much bigger purpose than any other enchanter or enchantress James—you are the only hope of the Pinnacle of Aries and to save all of us. I am really sorry about your mother, and I am sure she had her good reasons to give up her power stone by giving it to Burton. She never betrays us—I know her well."

The Davis brothers and James walked down the corridor to their scheduled classroom looking lost and shocked completely silent. Before they reached the classroom Henry broke the silence asking "James—how much do you know about your father?"

"Not a bit" replied James

"Has your mom told you anything about your father?" asked Mathew

"She doesn't say much but I am sure he was a loving and a caring man. Maybe she had her reasons to never talk about anything about him?"

"Did she mention a name?"

"Uh-ah—as I recall she always changes the subject when it comes to the subject about my father—I was not at the right age too to get anything more than what she told me." Said James calmly as they all walked into their noisy background with students still arriving and settling in chatting away.

It was the end of the class for the day of Professor Sisko and he walked through to go out of the classroom saying "James a quick word please!"

"Yes, Professor Sisko" replied James as he stood up and walked out of the classroom following Professor Sisko.

"James—I want to tell you something and I think it is important to help Laura."

"What is it Professor?" asked James with great interest.

"Laura's consciousness and spiritual self is with Burton and the only way to cure is your mother's power stone."

"Yes Professor I am aware of it—and I will somehow find a way!"

"I know you will James but there is another way!"

"What is it, Professor Sisko?"

"A power stone of your generation of your mother's side and a tear of the spirit dragon."

"But Professor—I do not know anyone in my family apart from..." James paused suddenly looking up at Professor Sisko with great shock.

"My aunt—Aunt Rebecca!"

Professor Sisko nodded slightly smiling approving James's response.

"But how can I go back—I mean we are still in the middle of a term to take permission?" asked James confusingly looking at the Professor.

"Leave that to me, James."

"Thank you, Professor Sisko!"

James and his friends were seated in the dining table, and a young enchanter wearing a black robe and cloak made with newspapers distributes the Phrontistery newsletter and newspapers.

"Are you sure your aunt will help you, James? Asked Mathew at the dining during lunch.

"She did everything to keep you away from knowing anything about the Pinnacle of Aries or her involvement with source powers you were confused about." Said, Henry.

"Or about your mother!" said Mathew.

"I know—but I got to try—for Laura," said James looking up at the brothers confidently.

"Well whatever you do we are with you James— for better or worse!" said Mathew with his brother nodding to agree with Mathew.

"Okay, James I got you permission for two days from Professor Galdor." Said Professor Sisko giving James a letter out of the classroom as they were standing about two steps away from students walking out of the classroom door and down the hallway.

"Phanto will take you to Mose."

"Thank you, Professor Sisko."

"James are you ready?" asked Phanto looking down at James with his usual pleasant smile.

"Yes" replied James holding three books in his hand.

"Give me the books—I will keep it at the quarters," said Henry.

"We'll see you on Friday James—let us know if you need anything," said Mathew calmly.

"How can I reach you?" asked James

"Oh yes—I almost forgot," said Professor Sisko putting his hand in his robe and taking out some reddish textured bird seeds.

"If you want to send a letter to your friends, I or anyone you wish to reach out to communicate anyone here—throw out some seeds and a messenger pigeon will come to you—tie the letter in its leg and just mention the name of the person you wish to send the letter to—Clear?"

"Yes Professor Sisko"

"Bye James," said the Davis brothers, and James walked away with Phanto.

Phanto and James walked through the busy town and through the pathway of the breathtaking mountains, flowers, and trees that changes shades of its trunk. They saw Gelda, the spirit of trees walking towards them with a calming smile.

"Hello James—I didn't see you at least once since I met you when you first got here!" said Gelda as she looked at Phanto and smiled saying "Hello Phanto!"

"Hello Gelda!" replied Phanto smiling back.

"How are you doing James?"

"I am fine—thank you"

"It's still the middle of the terms is it not? Is everything alright?"

"Yes—James is going to pick up some things he needs." Phanto replied.

"Oh I see—well then I wish you a safe journey and hoping to see you soon in the land of Aries."

James and Phanto walked up to a stone wall with a small wooden door with creeper plants grown all over the wall. Phanto knocked on the door and the door opened was opened by Mose and looked at Phanto and James.

"Then James—Good luck with getting that power stone—I will see you on Friday," said Phanto and walked away.

"Come on in lad! Said Mose as he pulled him inside his little cottage-like house closing the door saying "I thought I don't have to pull you in like cattle same as last time—how much can a great enchanter be lost ch!" wobbling towards James.

"I apologize I thought you didn't know why we are here." Said James looking at the midget man.

"Of course I know lad—no student can pass the gates of the Pinnacle of Aries through me, and without the approval of the Phrontistery. Now—go stand there and say the town of residence and say raferogus." Said Mose pouring some of that glowing sand to James's Palm.

"River Bay raferogus" in a flash he was right in front of the stone wall where everything strange just began. He walked through the woods and sights the house of Mr. and Mrs. Walsh at a distance.

Just then he remembered what on earth he is going to tell them especially to Mr. Walsh and in the strangest clothes as he was wearing a black robe and a green cape. He ran around the house making sure no one sees him through the windows and climbs up the ladder and pushed the window up of his room. He got into his room and quickly changed clothes to an old sweater and pair of jeans. It does not look the exact match for the fine polished black shoes and black socks he was wearing. He climbed out of the window and down the ladder running to the front of the house to walk to the entrance door knocking on the door just the way it's supposed to be to enter a house.

Mr. Walsh opened the door and his relaxed face changed to shock, and heard Mrs. Walsh walking down the stairs in a rush as she looks at James full of surprise.

"Oh James—my boy—where have you being?" asked Mrs. Walsh as she came running towards him and hugged him tightly. James could see how unhappy it is for Mr. Walsh to see his return frowning at him with great rage.

"Come in—let me get you some tea." Said Mrs. Walsh taking James inside the house. Ciara ran downstairs in a pink puffy dress with white stockings and shoes with a stuffed animal of a unicorn holding tight to her chest. She looks at James in astonishment and suddenly ran back up the stairs without saying a word.

"Aunt Rebecca I am here to speak to you about something important!" said James seated at the round white table near the kitchen without Mr. Walsh around.

There was not an ounce of curiosity in Mrs. Walsh's face as she was pouring black tea from a ceramic white teapot into a porcelain cup. She finished pouring a cup of tea and looked up at James saying "I know where you were James!"

"Why did you hide it from me? Who I am and who my mother is—who we are?"

"Is there an oath I've taken which I am not aware of to tell you everything that I know?"

"No—but I trusted you as family." Said James looking surprised at his aunt's response.

"That's exactly why I protected you!"

"Protected me! By hiding who I am and where I am supposed to be?" exclaimed James.

"Stop reacting James—you don't understand the kind of danger you are into once you are exposed to your true identity."

"I know the danger—I have come in contact with him—Burton!" said James courageously.

"That's enough!" shouted Mrs. Walsh.

"Listen to me James—you don't have anything to do with that evil man who killed…" she suddenly stopped saying a word further looking at James with great shock.

"My mother?" asked James calmly.

Mrs. Walsh stood up and walked up to the window quickly looking outside covering her mouth with her hand and whimpering.

"Aunt Rebecca—I know everything that happened, and I also know what I intended to do being who I am— Please—You got to help me!" said James walking and standing behind her.

Mrs. Walsh shut her eyes and took a deep breath opening them still looking outside the window.

"What do you want James?"

"Your power stone—my friend she is…"

While James was explaining Mrs. Walsh turned towards James saying "You don't understand what it means to protect your family—I failed to protect my sister and I can't let you do this—Joanne will never forgive me if something happens to you!"

"Aunt Rebecca I understand you're worried about me—but if we don't stop him he could destroy all of us—mother's power stone is in the wrong hands."

"Does Uncle Patrick know about who you are?" asked James

"No—the reason why I wanted a life away from the Pinnacle of Aries is to be away from the threats of that evil man. I wanted to live away from that life and protect Joanna—so I married to a man who has nothing to do with who we are."

"Why did mother give up her power stone?"

"I don't know James! I was not aware her power stone was gone—all I knew was that she did not survive—and she refused to be away from that dangerous life.

"So you did not want me to know about who I am or my mother because you wanted a life away from the Pinnacle of Aries isn't it?"

"Family comes first James! You will understand when you are older." Replied Mrs. Walsh calmly.

"Please let me have your power stone—I promise nothing will happen to me." James pleaded.

Mr. Walsh walked in saying "So James—how do you do to manage yourself—including the past few months?"

"Well—I   I work at a shop that belongs to my friend's father."

"I didn't know you had friends around here!" said Mr. Walsh with full of disbelief

"He is not here—I mean a childhood friend when I was living with my mother."

"That young huh? Those are some fine shoes you got there for a boy working in some shop!" said Mr. Walsh sarcastically looking at his well-polished black shoes.

"Patrick dear—that's enough drilling the boy—James why don't you go and freshen up a bit, I will prepare some lunch." Said Mrs. Walsh watching James walk through the doorway and up the staircase.

James climbed halfway up the stairs and he could hear Mr. and Mrs. Walsh talking a bit loud in a tone of a mild argument. James walked up the stairs and to his room. He sat on his bed relaxing and thinking about how he can get his aunt's power stone. He saw a corner of a letter underneath his pillow. He put his hand underneath taking out the folded letter and to see it was the letter he got inviting to the Phrontistery. He read the blue handwritten words that say "Find your purpose and do what is right!"
"I will" whispered James with great determination.

It is supper and Mr. and Mrs. Walsh, James, and Ciara are seated at the small dining table. James looked at his aunt and she looked back at James both seemingly in some deep thoughts of their own. After supper and cleaning up Ciara was in bed with Mrs. Walsh reading her a story and Mr. Walsh watching TV downstairs. James waited till Mrs. Walsh walks out of her daughter's bedroom leaning on the banister of the mezzanine upstairs.
Mrs. Walsh walked out of the room slowly closing the door of her daughter's bedroom making sure she doesn't wake up.
"Aunt Rebecca—can you please consider what I've told you about your power stone." Asked James as she walked past him through the mezzanine.
"I am sorry James I need some time to think about it!"
"But I've only got time till noon the day after tomorrow." Said, James
"James—it's almost fifteen years since I've had anything to do with it."
"That's alright Aunt Rebecca—if it's lost its power I just got to renew it from the Phrontistery."
"What else do you know after you went to the Pinnacle of Aries?" asked Mrs. Walsh curiously.
"I know enough—but there is one thing I want to ask you!" said James
'What is that?"
"Who is my father—have you met him?"

Mrs. Walsh nodded tight-lipped saying "Your mother was very closed up a bit too closed up especially about your father—she refused to even tell a name when I asked her."

"Can you please give me your power stone Aunt Rebecca—I promise I will bring it back to you and you won't regret giving it to me!"

"Let's talk about it tomorrow—why don't you get some early shut-eye with the long day of traveling," said Mrs. Walsh wanting to distract from the subject.

The next day morning James was up with a sleepless night thinking about how he can convince his aunt to give him her power stone. He heard a hard three bangs on his bedroom door and he got out of bed and walked up to the door to open it. It was Mr. Walsh and he walked into his room looking at him displeased.

"Sorry If I wake you up James—I want to speak to you before your aunt wakes up."

"What is it, Mr. Walsh?"

"Why are you here James?" asked Mr. Walsh frowning giving an obvious expression he is not satisfied with James's arrival.

"I came to take some of my things." Said James with a soft voice.

"Well—how long will you be here?"

"Planning to leave before noonday after tomorrow."

"Okay—well then make sure you don't leave anything behind." Said Mr. Walsh as he walked towards the door and turned around before he steps out of the room.

"If there is a possibility try to make that day after tomorrow to a day shall we? Or the earliest as possible—and your aunt don't have to know about this conversation." He walked out of James's bedroom closing the door behind him after the unpleasant conversation. James always knew he was the detestation for Mrs. Walsh even though he was their only nephew.

He waited till Mrs. Walsh woke up and all were downstairs with Mrs. Walsh fixing breakfast, Ciara ready for school, and Mr. Walsh ready to go for work. It was the perfect time for James to sneak into the master bedroom and he slowly walked into the room. It had a queen-sized bed with white and beige rich bed sheets, pillows and bed covers and a vintage table lamp, alarm clock on the right side hardwood bedside cupboard and a hardcover book, a cosmetic body lotion, and an old push-button telephone on the left. There was a tall three-door wardrobe in the corner of the bedroom. James quickly opened the door of the wardrobe and looked for the power stone underneath the neatly folded piles of clothes on each shelf. He opened the next door and it was a row of shirts belonging to Mr. Walsh hanged with three shelves underneath with two pairs of leather shoes. He opened the third door and it was some two evening gowns and her aunt's wedding dress hanged with steel hangers. Underneath the dresses were two shelves with a pair of walking shoes, two pairs of flat women's shoes, and a pair of evening high heels. He put his hand behind the line of shoes and he felt a metal jewelry box, and as soon as he took it out of the shelf he heard footsteps walking up the stairs. He let go of the jewelry box and close the opened doors of the wardrobe. There was a shadow of someone walking towards the room almost to enter the bedroom. James hid underneath the bed and saw Mrs. Walsh's feet walking to the wardrobe. She sat on the bed dialing some number on the telephone and heard her speaking on the phone.

"Hello Suzanne—how are you doing?" said Mrs. Walsh speaking to a woman named Suzanne except James was not sure if she is the same person who was her mother's best friend.

"That's great Suzanne—I am sorry I couldn't speak to you for almost three weeks I was caught with some things." Listens to her response and continues

"Listen I got to tell you something important—It's James—He didn't run away to just find any kind of life— he went to the Pinnacle of Aries." Listens to her response and replies saying

"Yes—Yes I know he would find out eventually—but he is here asking for my power stone! He says one of his friends needs it, and I am very sure that it's for something done by Burton." She listens to her and says with a soft voice "Suzanne—I am worried—I am afraid if I will lose everything like Joanne." Listens to her response and continues.

"I know—but if I saved her that night from Burton he will surely hunt me down—It's only my power stone and Joanne's is left in our generation."

James could not resist the amount of anger and hurt he felt having to hear that she did not help her mother to save herself. At the same time, he has to keep completely silent to make sure his aunt won't catch him underneath the bed, and as he tears with emotions and breaths heavily covering his mouth with his hand to avoid the sound of his silent sobbing and breathing. He carefully slides out of the bed from the opposite side his aunt is seated and quickly runs out of the room quietly as she was busy with the phone call.

He walks to his bedroom locking himself in and kneels down crying hard letting out his emotions of anger and pain.

"Spirit dragon please help me to find the power stone I don't want to stay in this house a day longer—please master—Guide me."

He was lying on his bed thinking and slowly fell asleep tired after a strong emotional moment of tears and rage. A dream appeared with the background of yellow light like watching through a pair of yellow lensed glasses of him walking to the aunt's bedroom from his room. He walks up to the wardrobe opens the door of the side the gowns were hanged and crouches down on the floor. His hand reaches to the mental jewelry box behind the pairs of shoes and opens it. The interior of the box had a red satin and a glowing power stone that brightened with a strong glow making the vision completely white and blank. James quickly woke up opening his eyes hearing the knocking of the door and the voice of her aunt.

"James—you haven't had anything all morning and it's almost noon."

"I will come downstairs" replied James reluctantly.

He walked downstairs and saw a man wearing a black trench court and grey old English-style suit and a hat talking to Mrs. Walsh in the living room. They were speaking about some house and their value. He thought it is the perfect time to look for the power stone in the metal box. He turned around taking two steps upstairs and stopped hearing the distracting conversation.

"It is certainly a high valued land—I suppose some renovations to the house could bring up some good value to negotiate." Said the man.

"Yes—we haven't visited there since my sister passed away."

"Are there any other parties involved—such as someone who holds the transfer on death deed?" asked the man.

"I am afraid not—but there is a trust will to have the property to her son as a beneficiary until he comes of age, but He passed away in a fatal accident."

"Oh, I am extremely sorry to hear that Mrs. Walsh—I hope you do not misunderstand what I am about to ask—I have a distant relative in this side of town and I was told that you have two children is that right?"

"Oh yes—after my sister's son passed away we adopted a child of the same age—I didn't have my daughter then and the only bundle of joy was our little James."

"I understand—alright then Mrs. Walsh I shall expect a call from you soon after a ready for sale land and a renovated house." Said the man standing up and hearing his footsteps walking towards the entrance door. James ran upstairs hearing his aunt say "Yes—thank you, Mr. Carter."

Before the man left the house he turned around to Mrs. Walsh asking her in the most formal manner. "One more thing Mrs. Walsh—I assume you have the required papers certifying the death of your sister's son— am I right?"

"Yes certainly"

"Very well then—good day to you Mrs. Walsh," said the man as he stepped out of the house and Mrs. Walsh closed the door lost in deep thought.

James took a deep breath and walked downstairs pretending to be fully unaware of what his own aunt had done all along who was the only family to him and his mother.

"Good afternoon James—shall I get some tea?"

James nodded striving to smile as she smiled back and walked into the kitchen. James followed her into the kitchen and looked upstairs as he passes the staircase with the need of the power stone sweeping in his mind.

"I will be in the backyard if you need me James—I got some new seeds to plant in the garden."

James nodded with a mild smile watching her walk to the kitchen and through back door. As an enchantress of Gravel, she could easily bloom the roses within a day. But she does nothing that involves any of her born source powers to live in the most normal life which a person could possibly imagine. It is the perfect time to look for the power stone, as the door closed behind her as stepped to the backyard James left the teacup on the round table and ran up the stairs. He could see Mrs. Walsh busy doing her gardening from the window of her bedroom. He opened the wardrobe and took the metal Jewelry box hidden on the lower shelf and opened it. It was a grey stone that looks nothing more than an ordinary slate rock. He took the rock out of the box and kept the steel box behind the shoes and closed the wardrobe door carefully without making the slightest sound. He looked outside the window and Mrs. Walsh was busy preparing the flower bed with a garden trowel. He quickly turned around to walk out of the bedroom and his aunt was standing staring calmly right outside the bedroom door. The power to travel with source powers of Gravel is one of the highest skills of an enchanter. . It is obvious she got the mastered skills with her sources powers and uses it if it's necessary.

"What are you doing here James?"

"Nothing I was just—um." Hiding the power stone in his palm behind his back.

"What have you got there?" asked Mrs. Walsh without an ounce of surprise.

"Nothing"

"Give it back James—you don't want to do this."

"No!" James shouted.

She ran towards him he jumped up to the bed pushing her and ran out of the room. She fell on the edge of the bed and to the floor and got up to chase him. He ran to his bedroom and locked the door and she banged on the door shouting at the top of her voice saying "James— open this door—don't you play with me—you don't know what I am capable to do. Do hear me—James!"

He changed to his uniform and took a pen and paper on his desk and wrote

"Phanto please help I have to get back to the Phrontistery soon."

He threw some seeds out and grew some branches from his powers through the window securing his bedroom door. She was hitting the door with something hard, and the door was ready to tear off but with the strength of the branches holding the door, it is difficult to hinder. He sighted the beautiful red pigeon flying towards his window and landed on the window frame. James rolled the letter and he saw a climber plant string on the bird's leg, and as soon as he kept the letter on the pigeon's leg the climber plant string wrapped the letter on its own.

"Phanto," said James to the bird and it flew away.

He got up on the window frame stepping on the tree branches that are grown through the window holding

the bedroom door. He stepped onto the ladder leaned next to the wall right next to his bedroom window

outside. James quickly stepped down a few steps and when it was close and safe enough he jumped to the

ground. He ran towards the wood and Mrs. Walsh ran out of the house just a few feet away from him. James

ran into the woods as fast as he can and his aunt chasing him. He sighted Phanto top riding a beautiful black

horse with wide black wings in the middle of the forest looking fierce at Mrs. Walsh.

"James stop—don't do this—don't you understand that family comes first!" Shouted Mrs. Walsh and James

stopped and turned around before he climbed up on the beautiful creature to join Phanto. He looked at Mrs.

Walsh and said "Yes—you are right!—family do comes first."

Phanto helped James to get up on the horse and flew away swinging its long black wings leaving Mrs. Walsh

helpless as she stomped her foot on the ground with towering rage.

Chapter Eight: The Acceptance

The horse flew up on the beautiful bright sky hearing the swing of the strong massive wings.

"Hold on tight James!" said Phanto as the horse flew turning and angling to the left. The horse landed

somewhere in the middle of the forest with Mose standing and seems like he was waiting for their arrival.

"Sorry to keep you waiting Mose!" said Phanto as he got down from the horse.

"Oh no—you didn't take long."

Mose walked close to the horse and rubbed its face "How are you my ladybug?" Said Mose and he walked

up and Phanto slightly bends holding his palms to Mose while the midget man gave a handful of glowing

sand.

"Stand here James," said Phanto pointing right in front of him, and after James was standing on the spot

Phanto threw the sand to their feet saying "Aries raferogus."

In a flash, they were at the Pinnacle of Aries and James felt so glad and relaxed feeling home.

As they were walking Gelda walked up to them smiling as the dried leaves drag behind her slowly as she

takes her steps towards them.

"Welcome back James—you are sooner than I expected."

"Yes, I got my things and decided to arrive today itself."

"Rebecca is never pleased to do anything on behalf of anybody—same as the old days!" said Phanto looking

at Gelda.

"Oh—she's too self-centered to be an enchantress! Are you alright James? Asked Gelda.

"Yes I am fine"

"We should get to the Phrontistery." Said Phanto looking down at James.

They were walking to the Phrontistery through the magical landscape that leads to the town.

"Do you know my aunt Rebecca?"

"Oh yes—but she was nothing like your mother."

"What do you mean?"

"She cares only for herself—no student could complain about her—one bad blow she awaits for revenge for the one who complains" Said Phanto.

"I am not surprised!"

"Is there anything you want to tell me, James?"

"I heard she was speaking to someone on the phone. The day Burton attacked my mother—my aunt refused to help her to save herself." James replied disappointed.

"Not all have the greatest power of one's self and it is none other than a person's heart. The good ones always receive more blessings than one could imagine. "

Phanto and James walked into the Phrontistery towards the hallway and walked up the stairs. Mathew and Henry saw James and walked with great excitement to see their friend again.

"James—you are back!" said Henry

"Is everything alright? I thought you will be back tomorrow—did you get the power stone?" asked Mathew curiously.

"Yes, I guess it needs to be renewed."

"Well—before we attend to the power stone why don't you meet Professor Galdor—he is expecting to speak to you once you return." Said Phanto and walked with a pleasing look.

"Ah James come in dear boy!" said Professor Galdor.

"I was told that you asked help by reaching Phanto—are you alright?"

"Yes sir—I am glad to be back and I got the power stone."

"That is wonderful but what happened back at home James?" asked Professor Galdor looking over his glasses.

"I wouldn't call it home sir!"

"Well, why in God's name do you say that?"

It's my aunt—she betrayed me all this time. I heard her speaking to someone and that she avoided helping my mother from the attack."

"I always had my doubts—that approves it. Typical Rebecca Spinner I should say!"

"Sir—I can't believe she did this—I trusted and loved her just like my mother."

"James—in this Phrontistery we have three congresses, and in this congress, we are all alike as a family with the born power of Gravel, Welkin, and Adam's Ale. But not all in the congresses are true enchanters or enchantresses in their hearts. The same way no matter where ever we go there is always a difference in one to another—even family."

James was listening to Professor Galdor and looked down in great disappointment.

"You always stay focus on what you have to do—listen to your heart and believe in yourself. Your aunt is not a bad person James—but she is not brave as your mother so she hides and runs away from her challenges then facing them. Our role is to forgive—to embrace love and kindness. Your mother gave up her power stone—but we trust her and we know it is not to betray us."

"But why did she do that sir? She could have fought back with her power stone." Said James as he looked curiously at Professor Galdor,

"James—your mother could have attacked and taken back her power stone, but if she did that you will not be existing by now." Replied Professor Galdor.

"Why is that sir?"

"The human world is different and very limited with the source powers to fight a large number of those evil witches and Burton. You were held by the witches at your childhood house, and the power stone can be taken. Unfortunately time was not sufficient to fight alone to save you. Therefore she gave up the power stone and saved you protecting you from the evil. She knew you will one day be a greater enchanter."

"How did you get to know this sir?" asked James shocked with what he was hearing.

Professor Galdor open a drawer and took out a heavy vintage book keeping it noisily top of the table. He turned the dark green vintage hardcover, and took an old letter inside it. He looked at the letter and handed it over to James looking at him over his glasses.

Dear Professor Galdor,

I am writing to express my sincere apology for having to cause much danger in the future by not being able to protect my power stone. I have no right

in providing an excuse for such a damaging act. I am trusting you will not fail to understand that my son James Spinner will be the future protector. In the world limited and helpless to defeat Burton, I had no option than to save my son who is your future blessed enchanter while I as his mother could not possibly sacrifice him. Therefore I am giving my son's future to your hands to bring him to the light of the great powers of the Pinnacle. I do not have much time left and until he comes to the rightful age he will be under the care of my sister.

Rebecca could have helped yet I do understand her to need to survive by avoiding Burton and his evil army of the Witchcrafts. Even if she did it was not a battle both of us could win.

Yours Faithfully,

Johanna S. Spinner

After reading the letter James heart was heavier as holding a cliff on his chest, but surely cleared James's doubts as he walked out of the quarters exhausted after a long day. James was walking towards the dining room Professor Cuppins's voice was heard in the background.

"James!"

He turned around and saw Professor Cuppins and Professor Sisko walking up to him.

"Come to my office tomorrow at eight first thing in the morning and we will look into the renewal of the power stone."

"Yes Professor Cuppins!" replied James as she walked into the dining room smiling graciously at James.

Professor Sisko held James's shoulder smiling down at him

"We appreciate your courage and commitment, James."

"Thank you, Professor Sisko."

James and the Davis brothers were seated in the noisy and crowded dining room with students seated at the long tables and spirit pixies at the table in front.

"James we checked for Darwin—he still hasn't returned after the day he had gone—the day of the attack." Said Mathew in a soft voice making sure nobody hears him.

"I wonder where he was trying to lead us at the forest." Said Henry curiously.

"That is not Darwin!"

"What—what do you mean James?"

"It's just an illusion—do you recall what Phanto said when we asked about the cave? My mother was trapped with the illusions to bring her to the house of the Spirit of Mortal."

"Are you saying what we saw was a trap?" asked Henry fearfully.

"James is right! What we saw was not Darwin leading us to find Laura it was just an illusion, and we were walking to a trap. Luckily Phanto saved us—but I wonder why Burton just gave up Laura."

"He didn't!" said James making the Davis brothers be fully shocked.

"Then who did?" asked Mathew.

"The Spirit Dragon!" replied James.

The next morning hearing the sound of morning bells ringing to a soothing melody. James got out of bed and rushed to be prepared for the day. He opened the wardrobe grabbing his books and the power stone and walked quickly out of the congress quarters and through the hallway.

"Stop right there James!" he heard a familiar voice at the back and he turned around it was none other than Wilbert. Wilbert looking envious as usual and two of his friends walked up to James.

"Where are you going, James?"

"Why would that interest you Wilbert?" asked James calmly

"Don't try to be too smart Spinner! What have you got there in your hand?" asked Wilbert looking at his clenched palm holding the power stone.

"Nothing!"

Wilbert pushed James making him fall on the floor hard with his books thrown all over the place but the power stone was held tight in his hand.

"What are you two idiots looking at? Go and get that thing off his hand!" shouted Wilbert at the two boys with him.

They walked up to James and tried to take the power stone from his hand, but James fought back as much as he could. Luckily Phanto walked through the hallways and sighted the trouble caused by Wilbert and his friends as usual.

"Stop! Please, if not I will have to complain to Professor Galdor!" shouted Phanto in a strong voice. It was hardly seen Phanto with a strong voice as such but his usual pleasant and calm voice. Wilbert and his two friends walked off, and Phanto helped James get on his feet.

"Are you alright James?"

"Yes—thank you"

James walked to Professor Cuppins's office knocking on the door and hearing to enter the room.

"Good morning James! What happened to you?" James looked down at his attire seeing his cape all crushed with the brawl in the hallway.

"Sorry Professor Cuppins—I forgot to hang the capes after I received them from the laundry."

"Hmm let's go attend to the renewal of the power stone—I don't want you to miss too much of your lecturers so let's try to get things done as soon as possible."

They quickly strolled to the lobby and the reception counter for power stone registrations and renewals.

"Professor Cuppins! How may I assist you this fine morning?" said the old reception elf lady.

"We need a renewal done to a power stone." Said Professor Cuppins taking the power stone from James's hand and handing it over to the reception elf lady. She took the power stone reaching out her gnarled and chalky hand.

"Oh this stone is off-glowed for a quite long time—I can tell."

The elf lady kept the stone at a sculptured hand made with a stone-like limestone or some igneous rock attached to the table. The hand held the stone tightly clutching from its finely sculpted fingers and the hand opened for the elf lady to take the stone out of the palm. She took a large book and placed the book in front of the sculptured hand. The hand turned the pages of the book and pointed to a row of details of the chart with all the owner's details, years, source power, and a number with two letters in front.

"Ah here it is— Rebecca Shirley Spinner—nineteen eighty-five—source power, Gravel and three hundred and eleven R S. Is there an owner or a family member who can authorize?"

"Yes—Mr. James Spinner."

The elf lady was surprised and looked down at the book reading the information and looked up at James. "Is this your mother's sister?"

"Yes"

"Write your name and sign here," said the old elf lady handing a feather and showing the blank space in the column next to the registration number of the power stone.

She poured a liquid from a tiny bottle into the power stone and slightly had a blend of color inside the stone. It changed colors from grey to green, red, orange, again red, and then to a yellow brightening its glow. The elf lady kept it back at the sculptured hand and it picked a feather underneath it on the table and wrote a renewal number front of James's signature as R.S. three hundred and eleven dash one. The power stone was glowing and lifelike which was handed over to Professor Cuppins by the elf seated at the counter.

Professor Cuppins turned around and gave the power stone to James looking at him smiling calmly.

"Professor Cuppins—what should I do next?"

"Now you save your friend!" said Professor Cuppins smiling at James.

"Come on let's get you to the hospital."

Just as they were about to leave Henry and Mathew came running to the lobby unknowing about Professor Cuppins's presence. As soon as the Davis brothers sighted Professor Cuppins they walked up to them then running and quiet as Professor Cuppins looked at them displeased.

"What are you two doing here?" asked Professor Cuppins.

"Sorry Professor Cuppins—we came to check on James—we—um." Mathew tried giving a helpful excuse for their arrival to the lobby.

While Mathew was having a tough time explaining themselves, Professor Galdor and Professor Sisko walked up to them.

"I assume everything is fine with the renewal?" asked Professor Galdor

"Yes sir!" replied Professor Cuppins with a steady voice.

"Are you boys here for any matter?" asked Professor Galdor.

"We just came by to check on James sir—will get back to our classes at once."

Responded Mathew reluctantly.

"Well if you children are willing to come along—maybe you could join us to go to the hospital." Said

Professor Galdor knowing exactly what the Davis brothers wanted.

"Can we—sir?" asked Henry excitedly looking at his brother.

"Let's go we cannot be late," said Professor Galdor as the three professors, James and the Davis brothers

walked towards the main door of the Phrontistery.

On the way to the hospital, James was in a deep thought walking through the pathway with tall trees on

either side with their leaves change to green-yellow, and brown planted with the powers of Gravel.

"Sir—can Laura be cured today itself?" asked James

"I am afraid not dear boy— the Power stone will need a full day, besides you should find a way to get a tear

from the almighty Spirit Dragon."

"Yes sir!"

They walked through the hospital and stopped around the bed Laura was lying down completely

unconscious and no different from the day of the attack.

"Come here James," said Professor Galdor asking James to stand on the side of the bed.

"Now keep the power stone on her chest and holding stone you have to say find the conscious of this rightful

being." Explain Professor Galdor with Henry, Mathew, two professors, and a spirit pixie at the hospital

looking at them curiously.

James kept the power stone on her chest and its glowing was brightening on and off.

"Find the conscious of this rightful being!" said James.

The power stone changed from yellow to green and red with images of Laura with her family back at home,

some pages of books or readings, times with James, Henry, and Mathew.

"Now we have to wait till the power stone finds her conscious and you have to get a tear of the spirit dragon through your born divine powers." Said Professor Galdor.

James and the Davis brothers were back at the Phrontistery and walked through the hallways.

"I will have to visit the Spirit Dragon and we will have to go to a place no one is around"

"How about the quarters? I am sure by now all the students would be in classrooms!" suggested Henry after thinking about a few seconds.

"Yes—that is a good idea."

They walked to the Gravel quarters and looked around where there was just one student who walked out and closed the narrow door of his belongings and shower room. They stopped near James's bed to pretend that they came only to pick up something. As soon as the boy left the quarters James leads them to the narrow door to his belongings behind his bed hood.

"Come in here—no one will see us if anyone walks into the quarters."

James turned the doorknob and pushed the narrow door inwards and they sighted was more than just a wardrobe and never flowing bathtub. It was the spirit dragon just standing and looking at the three calmly.

"Is—it that—the—spirit dragon?" asked Henry full of fear and about to cry and pass out.

"Master!" said James shocked with the presence of the spirit dragon in the quarters.

The head of the spirit dragon was almost touching the ceiling and its massive wings were folded backward and touches the floor. Its enormous tail was curled along the ground almost near the entrance door. James asked everyone to walk into the room and closed the door behind him.

"Master I cannot believe my own eyes—is that really you!" said James in utterly amazed.

"Yes James—I am here." said the Spirit Dragon graciously.

"Uh—is it normal that my brother and I can see the Almighty Spirit Dragon too?" asked Mathew looking confusedly at James and the Spirit Dragon.

"Yes—you are two great friends and there is nothing wrong in trusting the ones with you. So I believe it does not matter that I come before all of you to guide your dear friend James."

"It is an honor to meet you Spirit Dragon!" said Henry bowing his head with respect.

James was confused about the Spirit Dragon appearing openly in the quarters and visible to Henry and Mathew without any reason at all.

"I am here to give you something important James—I gave some thought to it and I decided it is good to have her with you."

"Who?"

"Your mother"

"My mother? But how?"

"I have the power to bring her to you but I will need your aunt's power stone to do that!"

"But what about Laura?" Henry asked anxiously.

"We have to cure Laura first Master!"

"You need a drop of my tears don't you?"

"Yes, we do."

"Give me the power stone I will strengthen its power with a tear and give it back to you. After curing Laura I will bring back your mother to you—but I will need the power stone."

Said the Spirit Dragon calmly.

"Let's go get it!" said Mathew about to open the door and run off to the hospital to bring the power stone.

"Wait!" cried out James stopping Mathew.

"Why did you decide to bring my mother back using powers?"

"She will help you James—and guide you!"

"How will she guide me, master?"

"Her powers of course!" said the spirit dragon. James looked into the Spirit Dragon's eyes and it was not the usual eyes with kindness and empathy but eyes with the presence of danger and a feeling of evil.

"What powers does she have?" asked James curiously

"The blessings of the Spirit Dragon!"

"That means you—isn't it master?" asked James watching and studying the movement of the eyes of Spirit Dragon being narrowed looking at James as he reassures what powers his mother held.

"Yes, James—Mine!"

"James, what is wrong with you? The Spirit Dragon will help us—we can cure Laura and we can bring your mom back to you too." Said Mathew.

"If you don't believe me look into this puddle of water—and you will see for yourself." Said the Spirit Dragon splashed water from the bathtub at the back of its tail, and some water spilled on the floor right in front of James.

James stepped closer to the water puddle on the floor and looked into it and saw a woman recognizable as his mother smiling at him.

She spoke to him with the voice of compassion and it echoes around the room saying "My son—let me come back and I will protect you!"

"How can you come back to me mother?"

"Give aunt's power stone to the master and I will join you at the end of the Pinnacle—I will help you to cure your friend. We can unite and Laura will be able to be with all of you—fully in mind and body." She vanished from the water puddle leaving James confused and yet too emotional to refuse to bring her presence.

"What are you thinking James?" asked Henry curiously

James looked up at the Spirit Dragon in great surprise remained in his deep thought.

"Master—can you remember what you told me lastly about where emotions could take someone?"

The spirit dragon and the Davis brothers were looking at James fully confused not knowing what James was uttering about.

"James—I am unclear of your words!" said the Spirit Dragon.

"Yes of course—you are not my master and you are not the Spirit Dragon!" shouted James.

The Davis brothers remained shocked while speechless, and mostly Henry was in fear as usual. It was not the smooth energy at presence and honor having to meet and speak to the Spirit Dragon, but in a room with a great danger.

"James—you are just confused. All you need to do is accept the help I am about to offer and give me the power stone that belongs to your aunt"

"No—I am not confused and I know exactly who you are! My master guided me to accept the reality, not some illusion that is convinced by using my emotions."

"Yes I do recall—maybe I just changed my mind!" said the Spirit Dragon.

"Stop this Burton—show your real self and face me. Don't be a coward."

"I have to say James the more I see your bravery the more I adore you. You may consider me as your biggest fan." Said the Spirit Dragon with a sarcastic tone except for this time the calm and soothing voice turned to a husky voice of Burton.

The body that appeared as the Spirit Dragon is a weapon in a time like this, and Burton took full use of it. He raised the tail and swing across the room hitting James, Henry, and Mathew. All three of them were thrown against the wall and to the corner of the room falling hard onto the floor. James with great willpower and strength kept his palms flat on the floor pushing himself up to be on his feet. The two siblings are luckily in Adam's Ale having the powers to use the water to fight back. Burton picked James from its long rattle tail in the body that disguises the Spirit Dragoon wrapping him around and squeezing him tightly like prey caught to a bone-crushing serpent. James screamed in pain as the tail gets wraps around him tighter and tighter. Mathew remaining on the floor after the hard-hit stretched his arm and used his powers. A soldier made from the water holding out a long sword emerged and stood on the surface of the water in the bathtub behind the disguised body of the Spirit Dragon. The soldier from the water held its sword from both hands and stabbed Burton between the wings and to the back of the disguised body.

Burton screamed in pain and vanished by changing to a black smoke that went away through the ceiling. James fell on the ground released from Burton's stronghold.

"James!" cried out Henry as he and Mathew both ran towards James worriedly.

"James are you alright?" asked Mathew helping James to stand up.

"I am fine—thank you." Said James holding Mathew's shoulder and look at him with great appreciation.

"What are friends for!" replied Mathew.

"Now I wonder if there is anyone outside and if anyone heard any of this." Said Henry with a glance at the door.

James walked up and opened the door slowly looking out. There was a group of students' right in front of the door looking shocked with eyes wide and one whispering to the boy next to him.

"Where was the music coming from?" asked one of the boys looking fully confused.

"Music!"

James walked to the students and looked around the room finding the slightest proof of music to his ears. There was the music of a symphony orchestral music coming from inside the changing room. Henry and Mathew walked out and stood beside James listening in shock.

"Where is it coming from?" asked Mathew

"You mean it's not any of you playing the music on something?" asked one of the students.

James saw Professor Sisko in the entrance with his fingers moving to the melody of the music. He stilled his finger lowering his hand while looking at James, and the music stopped instantly.

"It is me—um—I mean—I play a tape recorder inside the room." The students were convinced but Henry and Mathew were staring at James with bewilderment.

"James the old-timey!" said one of the students as they walked by with the sarcastic remark and the rest of the students laughed.

James walked up to Professor Sisko saying "Thank you, Professor Sisko."

"I knew something would happen when we are keeping the only other power stone of your generation—I was always in a close watch since your return, and I heard a voice through the walls which were taking the attention of the students around the quarters. So I distracted them with some music—besides its symphony six by the best musical enchanter Ludwig Willian Brahms—a priceless masterpiece." Said Professor Sisko as he walked away.

Henry and Mathew walked up to James right after Professor Sisko left.

"James I think we should soon cure Laura and hand over the power stone to the Phrontistery to be fully guarded." Said, Henry

"Yes, you are right! Having the power stone out there in the open is risky for all of us." Said, James.

"But why didn't Burton just go to the hospital and take it? I am sure he has more than enough powers to do something like that." Said Mathew confused.

"Because my consciousness is also his target which can be controlled only by my mother's power stone and that can only be taken if I am off guard and fallen to his trap." Said James full of confidence.

"How do you know that precisely?" asked Mathew

"The Spirit Dragon advised me to never fall for illusions—what Burton plays is by building trust on illusions he creates, and if I do fall to any of them I will be fully under Burton's control. Once he takes my conscious it will be trapped like Laura's and it is a great danger as it will be used with my mother's power stone. He can't unlock all its powers without a rightful owner with the born powers of the spirit dragon." Said, James.

"James—how did you know it wasn't the real Spirit Dragon and everything said was a trap?"

"Because I was guided to accept the reality—the reality is that my mother is no longer alive, and no power could reverse it. She is gone and I have to accept it no matter how difficult it is before any danger comes through."

"You did the right thing James!" said Mathew holding James's shoulder.

"Yeah—I can't imagine what would happen if you believed it—and we are sorry for falling for it and trying to convince you, James." Said, Henry.

"It's alright I would have done the same thing if I wasn't guided by the master himself. Anyway let's go try to cure Laura now and I should go and ask a tear from the Spirit Dragon."

"We will leave you to it, James—we will be in our quarters if you need us." Said Henry and the two brothers left the Gravel quarter doors.

"Master!" said James softly.

James appeared right in front of the Spirit Dragon in a cave made with red stones with red pigeons around and flying in and out of the cave.

"How are you, James? I was eager to speak to you soon."

"I am fine master."

"I am truly proud of you young enchanter—you followed my guidance and did the right thing."

"I am grateful to your advice—Burton tries all ways to win."

"Your challenges are yet to come James—the more you master your skills and power it is a threat to Burton and his tribe. He will do everything under his power to remove you from the Pinnacle of Aries."

"I understand master!" said James bowing his head with an agreement to the master.

"Now let's save your friend." Said the Spirit Dragon.

The Spirit Dragon picked a pigeon sending it out of the cave through the entrance of the cave. The pigeon came back with a slightly opened green flower bud and dropped to fall on the Spirit Dragon's palm. A tear from a gracious eye of the Spirit Dragon was dropped into the flower bud and the petals closed together. The spirit Dragon gave the flower bud and James held it with both hands with great respect.

"Thank you, master."

"It's a pleasure to help you save the Pinnacle of Aries and its great enchanters. Now return to your friend and cure her. I hope she will quickly return to her body and mind to where she is supposed to be."

James was back in his quarters holding the flower bud in his hands.

Chapter Nine: Power or Wonder

James walked out of the quarter doors to find Henry, Mathew, Professor Sisko, and Professor Cuppins

waiting for him eagerly. Professor Cuppins looked at the flower bud James was holding in his hand with

great care. She touched his shoulder gently looking at him with a warm smile, not something very often from

her as she always looks too serious.

"Let's get to the hospital!" said Professor Sisko.

They stepped to the hospital door walking through the row of beds that was either side of the walking path.

The spirit pixies in the hospital were astonished and stares as the Professors and Davis brothers walk to the

helplessly unconscious Laura with James walking in front with a flower bud covering the Spirit Dragon's

tear. It is not unknown by the hospital or faculty staff that there is no other treatment apart from the power of

a Spirit Dragon's tear and a power stone of the only generation blessed by the powers of the Spirit Dragon.

A fairy spirit Pixie that flew through the window gave some herbal leaves to one of the spirit pixies in the

hospital. The tiny flying pixie sighted the presence of the Spirit Dragon's tear covered by a flower bud of a

kind that is only available in the spirit world of the Spirit Dragon. No enchanter, enchantress, or spirit pixie

had ever visited the land apart from the very first enchanter picked by Aries in history, the enchantress Mrs.

Johanna Spinner from the generation of the first enchanter in the bloodline with born blessings by the Spirit

Dragon, and now her son James Spinner.

The fairy pixie flew outside through the window and seconds after fairy spirit pixies were flying right

outside each window of the hospital watching James in great wonder. Professor Galdor and Phanto came

running into the hospital towards James.

Professor Galdor took the flower bud from James's hand in great respect and was amazed at the magical

presence from the Spirit Dragon's tear covered with a flower bud only seen in books and heard from his

childhood as it was taught to believe. He looked at James with eyes looking graciously at James with a slight

bow of appreciation.

"It is time to do the magic!" said Professor Galdor handing back the flower bud to James carefully.

Henry, Mathew, Phanto, Professor Cuppins, and Professor Sisko stood aside watching with great hope with three hospital spirit pixies standing next to them praying silently.

James slowly walked up to Laura to look at the power stone on Laura's chest, and as he leans forward he sees black smoke moving around inside the stone.

"Professor—the power stone—it's all dark!" said James worried looking at Professor Galdor.

"Don't worry dear boy—it means her consciousness is found in the place of evil."

James looked down at the flower bud in his hand and take it close to the power stone. He pours the tear angling the flower bud towards the power stone slowly. A petal of the power stone slights opened to let the tear pour down the petal and into the power stone.

"James now stands back," said Professor Sisko as the power stone brightens to a strong glow hard to watch from the naked eye. While all were looking at the beautifully glowing stone, the glow diminishes slowly bringing back a bit of the black smoke moving inside the stone.

"It's impossible!" said Professor Cuppins as the Professors looks at the stone in great shock and James, Davis brothers, and the hospital spirit pixies confused.

"What's wrong Professor? Why didn't Laura wake up?" asked James

"The presence of evil still prevails blocking the travel of her consciousness."

"What can we do Professor?" asked Mathew

Professor Galdor, Professor Cuppins, and Professor Sisko remained silent looking at the power stone.

"It needs more power!" said Professor Cuppins looking at James and Phanto.

"Quick! We need three source powers to strengthen the power stone. Three for source power hold the power stone." Said Professor Galdor as he stepped forward placing his hand on the power stone and giving force of his power.

"I can give for Adam's Ale." Said, Mathew

"I can for Gravel," said James.

The two boys stepped with great willingness to help Laura get back to her consciousness saved from the hold of Burton's power.

"No! Both of you—step back—it's too dangerous and powerful."

Professor Sisko stepped forward placing his on Professor Galdor's hand on top of the power stone.

"We need someone from Gravel!" said Professor Sisko looking worried at Professor Galdor.

"You've got one!" came a familiar voice from the side of the hospital entrance. All turned around and it was Professor Lansford walking fast towards them and looking at James in some thought.

"Professor Lansford! Oh, thank goodness." Said Professor Sisko and Professor Lansford placed his hand on top of Professor Sisko's hand.

"Alright—ready?" asked Professor Galdor looking at Professor Sisko and Lansford courageously.

"Now!" shouted Professor Galdor and the power stone struck a light bright from the sky as the light brightened the stone as strong as the light of the sun is right beneath their hands. A strong wind blew all over the hospital with Davis brothers, James, Professor Cuppins and Phanto covering to protect from strong light flashed from the power stone.

The wind stopped and the brightness of the light was slowly diminishes allowing all to open their eyes and let down their arms guarding the eyes. The hospital was a mess with white sheets blown all over the floor and little medicine bottles dropped for the strong wind caused by the strength of the power stone. Professor Galdor, Professor Sisko, and Professor Lansford removed their hands and stepped back. Everyone around watched Laura as she remained unconscious on the bed without any movement. After a few seconds she opened her eyes watching around her in great shock and breathing heavily. It was a moment of happiness and relief to the faculty management, James, Davis brothers, and the spirit pixies watching her hoping her consciousness to return to her. The fair spirit pixies were cheering, clapping, and giving the sweetest high-fives to each other.

Laura sat on the bed looking at James, Mathew, Henry, Professor Galdor, and then to Phanto and she recalled the last time she remembered was in the bell towers remembering she was attacked by Burton.

"Laura!" said James with great excitement

"Are you okay?" asked Mathew looking closely at Laura.

"Laura—say something!" said James concernedly

"You saved me! Oh, I can't believe it —I've got no words to say how grateful I am to be back."

"It's good to have back dear, but you have to thank your dear friend here who made things possible to bring you back to right self!" said Professor Cuppins with a glance at James touching Laura's shoulder as she looks at her with a pleasing smile.

"You should get some rest and from tomorrow you can go to your quarters and start to have your day as usual" Said Professor Galdor.

"May I start it from today itself, sir? I feel like I don't need sleep for a decade."

"Well—in that case, I suppose it's alright?" asked Professor Galdor looking at the hospital spirit pixie waiting he awaits for the approval of the spirit pixies. The spirit pixie nodded calmly with a smile giving Professor Galdor the approval.

"We should get back to the faculty." Said Professor Cuppins and the faculty management and Phanto left to go back to the Phrontistery.

Professor Sisko turned back looking at Laura saying with his usual friendly voice "Looking forward to seeing you in class Laura."

"Thank you, Professor Sisko." Said Laura.

Laura jumped out of bed in excitement hugging James, Mathew, and Henry as they were looking at her with a grin and Laura looking excited at them. Mathew and Laura looked at each other completely locked with their eyes. Henry and James noticed tightening their lips to hold back their laughter looking back and forth at the two lost in their world.

"Shall we get on with starting that usual day getting back to the Phrontistery?" said Henry sarcastically.

Mathew and Laura quickly came back to their right senses looking looked around at Henry and James fully embarrassed.

"Yes—we shouldn't be late for lectures!" said Mathew pretending as if nothing more distracted him differently and things are the same as it is for James and Henry.

The Davis brothers, James and Laura walked back to the faculty with Henry teasing Mathew after seeing his brother's moment of attraction to Laura.

"Shut up Henry!" said Mathew.

Two girls came running as soon as they saw Laura walking into the Phrontistery with her three friends.

"Laura! It's so great to see you" said one of the girls.

"It's great to be back!"

On the way to the lectures as scheduled Laura, James, and Davis brothers walked to the class. James was in deep thought in complete silence walking through the hallways.

"What are you thinking James?" asked Laura

"I was wondering where Darwin is and I didn't see Father Tolmen for days too."

"Father Tolmen had gone to attend to some of his matters—Phanto told me when I inquired about him." Said Mathew.

"You mean he is away from the faculty?" asked Laura

"Away from Aries!"

"What about Darwin?" Laura asked.

"Last he was seen by his home folks was the day of the attack to the Phrontistery." Said James looking at Laura as they all entered the class.

Father Tolmen's subjects were free due to his absence and James, Laura and the Davis brothers decided to go to the study room. While they were busy doing their revisions and studying their textbooks Mathew was thinking something looking curiously at James.

"What?" James grunted.

"I was just wondering maybe we should try to find out where Father Tolmen is— where he is or whatever he is doing could be something that relates to your mother or you."

"What makes you say that?" asked Henry

"The death certificate we found at his chambers of course! What business does he have to get a copy of the false death certificate of your mother and having it to be posted to him?" Said Mathew looking at James with great curiosity.

"Well giving a thought to it in that way I agree, and I also got something important to tell you all." Said Laura looking around at the Davis brothers and James.

"What is it Laura?" asked Henry

"When my conscious was held by Burton I remembered something last night. I saw a large bowl-like thing made in metal fixed on a tall stand and it looks like surrounded by blue flames all around it. I was taken and thrown inside the bowl and I spirit pixies just floating around with their eyes closed. It seems like they were barely alive and trapped with some great force inside the metal thing."

"Can you remember Phanto mentioned about how Burton trapped some spirit pixies?" asked James.

"But they were rescued by the management of Phrontistery and your mother." Said, Henry.

"Yes—but what if some trapped and couldn't be rescued till this day," James responded making a line between his dark eyebrows.

"What are we going to do?" asked Laura.

"We got to find Darwin first! I have a feeling he has something to do with Burton."

Professor Cuppins's class is as usual a bit boring yet the most informative to the ones who love to read like Laura. Some of the lessons are quite enjoyable to all students as a keen enchanter or enchantresses like James and the Davis brothers. But the lesson of this particular day was the best for all in general. The learnings of the wonders of science in nature and surroundings particularly the uniqueness in the Pinnacle of Aries is the best to learn. Therefore the lesson is not just books, talking, and classroom but a walk outside exploring the deep forest taken by Phrontistery itself. Phanto and Professor Cuppins made sure the lineup of the students is right looking if everyone is to start the tour. The students had a wood-covered notebook with its pages tied with a spiral made of a climber plant, and a feather to write down any important details.

"Thank goodness something adventurous after ages in classrooms." Said Mathew.

"I wish to agree but the adventure we encountered was an adventure of life and death—especially to James." Said Henry feeling bitterly afraid about going into the forest.

"Is everyone here?" asked Professor Cuppins checking to see if all joined the line to start the tour.

"Before we start—there are a few things that you have to keep in mind and adhere to. You all have to stick together and no one is allowed to take off of your own will without informing me or Phanto for any reason. Do not consume any fruits you come across that you don't know and do not touch or try to do anything if you see something unusual to explore without our permission. You are expected in your best behavior and keep in mind to concentrate the lesson well. There will be the main part of knowing the science of nature in your examinations at the end of the semester. Come along now!"

The students walked excitedly with Professor Cuppins and Phanto leading the class into the woods. They walked past the waterfall the covers the cave and no word was uttered about the house of the Spirit of Mortal as its history is buried to protect from the cave with casted spells. Passing a meadow of flowers that blooms with a glowing yellow, Professor Cuppins and Phanto stopped turning around to face the students. "Alright gather around please—these are called "Lampyridae flowers" and it's used to produce lanterns and lightings as the light drops seen in the Phrontistery. It is also used for casting solutions made to cure slight scratches for wings especially used by spirit pixie fairies. Further details refer to your textbooks." They walked through the trees with wild mushrooms mostly grown near the tree barks for the moisture of the ground.

After a certain distance of travel through the woods was another clear ground with light green grass and a stable filled with white horses that were bright and white as snow, with many grown ones and foals. Among these beautiful horses was also a type of horse that was no ordinary. There were brown horses with only their beautiful face and neck and the rest of the body were fully in leaves, long legs with a bundle of sticks, and wearing horseshoes made with metal. A long natural horsetail that looks brushed and perfectly in place. A man wearing a pair of leather cowboy boots and black pair of tight-fitting trousers, with a shirt and a jacket with sleeves like a dark green cape with high collars. He wore a brown cloak attached to his broad leather belt that had metal rings and a pouch that holds a knife at his hip. He wore a brown hat that shaded his eyes and was the sunlight fall on his pointy chin, square face, and thin lips. He was tall and walked calmly towards Professor Cuppins.

"Hello, Maverick." Said Professor Cuppins.

"Good day to you Professor Cuppins—Phanto!" said Maverick with his pleasant voice and country-like accent doing a quick head bow greeting with respect. Phanto repeated the same remaining silent but his pleasant smile and friendly bow say it all.

"Yes, this is the new batch of students for the year." Said Professor Cuppins.

Phanto walked into a separated long cottage and walked out bringing the beautiful black horse with wings that Phanto arrived to take James back to Aries the last time he left to his aunt's place to borrow her power stone but ended up taking it despite her agreement.

Professor Cuppins turned around to the students with Phanto standing a few steps back holding from its headcollar rope.

"Everyone this is Pegasus and the only spirit horse that could fly for miles or days. It can fly up to ten thousand feet. There is a difference in its body structure and bones where its wings have hollow bones that give its strength to cut through the strongest winds. The other spirit horses have speed and the same bone structure as a normal horse like the beautiful white ones we see around. Now—all of you will get a chance to go on a ride on Pegasus—pair up with one of your fellow students all of you."

The students excitedly paired up Laura with James and the Davis brothers as another group. The students get a ride around the forest and land right at the spot at the horse stable area in front of the Professor, Phanto, and Maverick which was the place it took off.

"You're up James!" said Phanto. Laura and James got up on the black beautiful creature as it stretches its wings and flew up distancing the ground more and more.

"Hang on tight Laura!"

"This is magical—the forest looks beautiful from above." Said Laura as she looks down at the landscape in a larger view from above in wonder.

The horse angled its wings and took off opposite to the direction it's supposed to ride.

"Where are we going?" asked Laura.

"I don't know!" said James with eyes of worry without the control of the horse.

It took them up the deep forest and from a certain point the entire land is covered in dark smoke, and Pegasus takes a curve right in front of the line that divides from the blackish smoke.

"What is that?" asked Laura shouting through the hard wind and looking back at the dark smoke.

"I don't know! But I am positive we were taken here to show the place."

They reached back to the spot they took off and Professor Cuppins and Phanto walked up to them looking worried.

"Goodness what took that long to return—I was starting to worry." Said Professor Cuppins.

"We are fine Professor!" said James as he got down from Pegasus.

Some students were teasing and making fun of Laura and James for their delay to arrive.

"What took so long you two? A secret adventure with a magical ride on Pegasus". Said one of the boys in a sarcastic voice as the rest of the students laughed.

"Are you two okay?" asked Mathew as he walked up to James with Henry.

"We are fine—but we were taken to see something very strange. This place is like a land of beyond that is full of darkness." Said Laura with curiosity.

"Full of darkness? What do you mean?" asked Henry

"We were taken somewhere through the deep forest and from a certain point—a black smoke covers the land entirely. It is—"

While Laura was busy explaining to the Davis brothers, James was lost in a deep thought frowning and looking down at the ground. Interrupting Laura's explaining James suddenly broke his silence.

"The end of the pinnacle!"

"What?" Laura asked, but the Davis brothers know exactly what James meant as they were with him when the whole incident took place.

"Are you thinking that's the place the illusion of your mother made by Burton spoke about?" asked Mathew curiously.

"Yes!"

"Seems like I've missed too many things during my deep sleep." Said Laura sarcastically and disappointed all at the same time.

"Let's ask about it from Phanto—he should be knowing about it!" said Mathew looking at Phanto who was helping a girl get on Pegasus for a ride.

"Did everyone take their turns to go on a ride on Pegasus? Asked Professor Cuppins and looked around for confirmation.

"Alright we will be moving on—everyone come along now! Oh and thank you Maverick, and do let me know the progress of Pepper! I am sure it will recover soon after the treatments given yesterday." Said Professor Cuppins as she looks at Maverick.

"Certainly Professor—see you around Phanto" replied Maverick and smiles at Phanto as he walked past Maverick.

They walked past the green meadows and trees and walked to the most beautiful lake which was the most breath-taking view. It was a large lake that is surrounded by wildflowers and bushes that had water lilies all over the lake. A girl was seated on the side of the lake with her legs in the waters wearing a wrapped skirt made with petals of water lilies, and hair long floating on the water seated on the ground with her feet touching the water.

"Can you call Esther for us please?" said Phanto to the girl.

She nodded and jumped into the water and her legs transformed to a mermaid tail as she dived deep into the lake. Esther swam up the surface of the water looking at Phanto and Professor Cuppins with a wide smile. Her beautiful upper half of the body showed out of the water till the white and grey scalps on her hips of the mermaid tail. She pushed her into the edge of the lake and she got out of the water her mermaid tail transformed into legs with a gown made with a large water lily bud. Her hair which is water flows beautifully in a fresh-looking white and blue with water lilies on her hair

"Oh, a lesson outdoors—it's great to see you all. I was waiting till this day comes to meet the new batch."

"Hello, Esther—you're looking lovely as always. I assume you must have received the message I sent on preparing the things I need for the lesson?" Said Professor Cuppins calmly.

"Certainly!"

"She looks hot!" said a boy at the back.

"Mr. Rodriguez I hope you haven't forgotten that you are required to be in the best of your behavior?" asked Professor Cuppins displeased.

"No Professor Cuppins" replied the boy apologetically.

Esther gave a handful of seaweeds to Professor Cuppins given by another mermaid who emerged to the surface of the water.

"Alright everyone—this is called Citricast weeds, and it will help you to hold your breath for an hour. But more than an hour of its reaction consuming a piece longer than an inch is not advisable and will be a risk to your life." Said Professor Cuppins as she and Phanto break the Citricast weeds into tiny pieces which are in dark reddish.

"How is that possible that one could survive without breathing for an hour Professor?" asked James.

"The Citricast weed will hold to build the carbon dioxide in your lungs and stops the need to exhale for an hour. The Citricast weed has the powers of Welkin and it is only found here in this lake which is under the protection of Esther."

"So does that mean the Welkin source powers can create Citricast Weeds?" asked one of the girls in the Welkin congress.

"No dear child—I am afraid not! You see some of the wonders in the Pinnacle of Aries are magic of nature. You all as the great enchanters and enchantresses one day have many capabilities and powers with the source powers you are born with—however, some things are just wonders of nature that can never be replaced." Said Esther calmly with a pleasing slight smile.

"Now everyone takes just one piece of the Citricast weed and eat it. Do make sure you chew it well to get the most out of its properties." Said Professor Cuppins as Phanto was holding out his palms together filled with pieces of Citricast weeds. All the students took a piece and chewed as instructed.

"Oh—it's so bitter!" said Henry with him and all the students chewed with faces of disgust with its bitter taste.

"What do you expect? A piece taste like shortcake?" asked Professor Cuppins sarcastically as Esther giggled softly.

"Line up everyone and jump into the water—one at a time please!" Said Professor Cuppins as Phanto had his piece and jumped into the water first.

All the students kept their notebooks and feathers on the ground and jumped one after another splashing water all over the ground with great excitement. Once they are in the water everyone can hold their breath just fine. The students were enjoying underwater and it was like a whole new world underneath. Corals and flowers are mostly lotuses that change color and texture just like the walls of Phrontistery all over the bottom of the lake.

"I forgot to tell you—you can also speak underwater as you do on the ground. The Citricast weed also allows you to hear and speak in the same frequency as you do out of the water." Said Professor Cuppins as the students listens fully astonished.

They start talking to each other in great excitement trying out the magic of the seaweed. The sound of the little chit chats gradually turned to a noisy background with Phanto and Esther looking at the students pleased with the excitement of the students.

"Silence please—do remember you are expected to be in the best of your behavior even underwater." Said Professor Cuppins yet calmly making it a slightly sarcastic comment.

The students swam seeing the beauty with shoals of fish, mermaids swimming around as they waved and lady mermaids giving flying kisses at the students. One beautiful mermaid passed Mathew as she looked at him shyly, and Mathew blushes and looks at her with eyes wide admiring her beauty. Laura observes it closely and looks mostly at Mathew and the mermaid lady and is surely displeased.

"Someone boiling underwater!" said Henry softly and sarcastically to James as they both laughed quietly. Professor Cuppins explains the plants, corals, and the types of fish exactly how it is an underwater trip no different from a field trip enjoying a magical yet rare moment of exploration.

Chapter Ten: Rightfully Owned

James climbed out of the water on his hands' knees with his friends Laura and Davis brothers along with the other students. The students were pleased with the field trip both on land and underwater. Finally, Professor Cuppins climbed out of the water with Phanto looking around at the students.

"Is everyone here?" asked Professor Cuppins.

All looked around nodding to Professor Cuppins confirming everyone is out from the lake, with water dripping from their hair, clothes, and body all soaking wet. Esther was still in with her mermaid tail in the water and the top half out of the beautiful female body out of the water. Professor Cuppins turned to Esther and nodded to her confirming something that was not aware by any of the students. Esther pushed a large wave of water larger than one found on the sea during stormy weather from her bare hands.

The wave flows to Phanto, Professor Cuppins, and the students and dragged each drop of water on the clothes, body, and hair as the wave slowly went back into the lake. The students, Phanto and Professor Cuppins were dry as if they were yet to get into the water just as the walls in the Phrontistery representing the Adams's Ale source powers. There was no sign of a water wave that had come off the lake and onto the ground, but dry dirt with plants and flowers without a single drop of water anywhere to be found.

"Wow! Did you guys see that?" said Henry while they all walked back into the Phrontistery.

"I know—it's incredible," said James.

"Finally! It's Friday and less homework since Father Tolmen is absent." Said Mathew.

"Yes—I want to know about Father Tolmen—I want to know if he has any communication with my aunt."

"Why you say that James?" asked Laura

"When I went back to my aunt to ask for her power stone—there was a lot of things I saw and heard which I wouldn't have dreamt in the worse nightmare," James said as he looked down in a complete disappointment.

Laura and Davis's brothers paused as James stopped walking along with them.

"What happened James?" asked Henry.

"My aunt lied to me all this time—she didn't help my mother through the attack even though she could, and she is trying to sell my mother's house by lying that I died in an accident."

"How did you get to know all this?" asked Laura

"I heard her speaking to my mother's best friend Suzanne over the phone—and I also heard her speaking to a man at her house about my mother's property which I rightfully own. I think he is related to some property business. She said that I no longer exist, and when the man inquired who I was that used to live with her for all these years—she–she..."

"What is it James—what did she tell him?" asked Laura looking at James angrily.

"She said I am a boy adopted to overcome her nephew's passing." Said James and Laura's anger turned to sadness as well as the Davis brothers.

"Don't worry James—I am sure we can all stop her from doing the wrong things. We will help you to do whatever it takes." Said Mathew.

"Yes—and I strongly think Father Tolmen has something to do with this," said Laura.

"It is also possible he is trying to find what your aunt is up to and to stop her from doing the wrong things to you. After all, you are a student here and the faculty will never let anything bad happen to you." Said Henry.

"But we don't know that for sure—so far not everything is as it seems!" said Laura.

"Yes—you are right—and I think we shouldn't speak to Father Tolmen about any of this until we get to the bottom of what he has to do with that death certificate we found in his chambers."

"What about Professor Galdor?" said Mathew suddenly but confident on what he uttered.

"What about him?" Henry asked turning to his brother.

"That's a great idea! He must be knowing where Father Tolmen is or something about him." Said James excitedly.

"If he questions your business finding of Father Tolmen's whereabouts—what exactly are you planning to tell him?" asked Laura curiously.

"I am going to tell him the truth—I am going to tell him what we found at his chambers"

"Are you sure—that's a good idea? Asked Mathew.

"Yes I know I can trust him—and we won't be in trouble. I promise!"

"Don't worry James—we trust you!" Replied Laura giving him an assuring smile.

The bells rang and they all walked into the Phrontistery, and James walked towards Professor Galdor's chambers.

James knocked on the door and he heard Professor Galdor's voice from inside the room.

"Come in!" James opened the door and walked in looking for Professor Galdor. He seems busy looking for something inside a large box with some capes designed slightly different from the capes of the faculty uniforms.

"Here it is," said Professor Galdor turning around and sees James.

"Oh hello James—this is the first uniform at the faculty, and we were planning to do something special to teach some history of the Phrontistery for the Founders Day next week." Said Professor Galdor as he went back to his seat made with strong tree roots, and cushioned with red feathers.

"So how may I help you in this fine afternoon?"

"I need to know something important sir!"

"Have a seat James." Said Professor Galdor and James looking slightly nervous sat on one of the visitor chairs

"What is it boy—is everything alright?"

"I want to know about Father Tolmen sir."

"I am happy to tell you whatever I know—what is it that you need James?"

"I was told he left for some matters—did he tell you why he left sir?"

"Yes—but May I dare to ask why you inquire about him?"

"I came across something very personal to me and I believe there is something to do with wherever Father Tolmen is right now."

"It is actually for a matter at the Phrontistery he is off to—only he, I, and Professor Cuppins know about the matter. We require a place to allocate a group of enchanters or enchantresses to search for the power stones that belong to the deceased enchanters and enchantresses—also the living but no longer at the Pinnacle of Aries. We found in our records that some of the power stones are not updated in our records till the present day. Therefore we believe that these power stones are out there in the human world that is no longer under our protection which is easily accessible by Burton and to the witchcraft tribe."

"What exactly can he do if Burton gets these power stones, sir?"

"Power stones are very useful to the Witchcrafts and to strengthen their powers used even after the rightful owners are deceased. Through the owners or someone that belongs to the bloodline of the generation the power stone can be used by taking over their consciousness. Having said that—there is another important fact that brought to our attention."

"What is that sir?"

"The deceased is not just of old age, but by taking over their consciousness to use the power stone— unconscious for weeks and months that no medicine or treatment could cure in the human world, and dies getting weak each day in their physical being. The enchanters and enchantresses away from the Pinnacle of Aries with the power stones are a target—and most of them are unaware of the fact that the strongest power stone is with Burton that could steal the consciousness of another."

"But we can cure them, right sir? My aunt's power stone—we succeeded to save Laura!"

"No James—Laura's powers are not yet embedded to a power stone. Most of our power sources are used only with the power stone, and we should know well how to use them. That is why with what happened back in history a student undergraduate will not receive his or her power stones until they've learned the basics, history, nature, source powers, techniques and so on."

"Why can't we save the ones with the power stones, sir?" James asked worriedly.

"Once the power stones are taken by Burton there is no reverse to save them—the only way is to bring the consciousness if the bodies are physically existing with life. There is a way to stop Burton and his tribe from taking the consciousness and misusing the power stones."

"How can we do that sir?"

"Taking away the immortal powers away from Burton and that removes the undead powerful witches from the witchcraft tribe that leaves them powerless to fight back—the existence of Burton with immortal power can be broken by your mother's power stone. The powers of an immortal can be used only with the absence of the Spirit of Mortal and can be broken only by a power stone of an enchanter or enchantress with born

blessings of the Spirit Dragon.”

“That is why Burton killed the Spirit of Mortal first!” said James frowning and surprised. Professor Galdor

nodded to confirm James’s conclusion.

“But sir—how can Burton use my mother’s power stone? She is no longer alive.”

“The night your mother was killed is the first death caused by Burton weakening the physical being for days,

weeks, and months by taking the consciousness to use the power stone. Your mother lived unconsciously for

six months after the day of the attack. The consciousness will never die as it lives in the power stones. We

tried finding your aunt’s power stone but she hid everything her identity and her power stone out of fear for

her life.”

“How does Burton find the power stones in the human world?” asked James curiously.

“The visions of the Witchcrafts strengthens by the powers of your mother’s power stone of course.”

“Sir—my aunt’s power stone was not used for years and my mother’s is with Burton—how did you find

me?” Professor Galdor looked over his glasses looking into his eyes.

“Your purpose was written the day you were born James—and a legend that awaits to be written as the only

son of the Enchantress Joanna Shirley Spinner.”

“I understand sir! Did Father Tolmen say where he is off to?” asked James suddenly changing the subject.

“Well—he did give an address of a person he wished to see to go look for some places and hear some deals

for a place that suits our requirement.” Professor Galdor opened a drawer on the side of his office table and

gave a piece of paper with a handwritten address.

“Thank you, sir.” Said James as he stood up to leave.

“James” called out Professor Galdor before he opened the door. He turned to Professor Galdor saying “Yes

sir?”

“Is there anything else you need to tell me?”

James looked at Professor Galdor speechless and refused to say “No sir!”

Laura, Mathew, and Henry were seated in the study room, and Laura as usual sucked into a book while Davis brothers playing chess.

"Hi James—did you speak to Professor Galdor?" asked Mathew

"Yes I did"

"What was his reaction when he heard we sneaked into Father Tolmen's chambers?" asked Laura.

"Actually I didn't utter a word about it."

"What do you mean?" asked Henry confused.

"Father Tolmen had gone to find a place for a requirement of the Phrontistery—to bring back and protect the power stones from the human world to the Phrontistery. Professor Galdor gave me an address Father Tolmen had given him before he left." James showed the piece of paper taking it out of his side pocket in his robe.

"Which means Father Tolmen has nothing to do with the death certificate of your mother?" asked Henry confused.

"Which mean he literally has something to do with it without Professor Galdor's knowledge!"

"I don't understand James—what makes you say that?" asked Laura.

"James is right! It's not like Father Tolmen does not know what really happened to Mrs. Spinner." Said Mathew confidently looking at James.

"Well thinking about it in that way I guess I feel the same." Said, Laura

There is a question that's still unanswered—what is Father Tolmen's business with the false death certificate? I mean faculty won't need some false record, but it could also mean he is trying to find the truth as a help to you—after all, she did give the faculty a reason to come after her avoiding to help her own sister" said Henry curiously.

"That's what we got to find out!" Said Laura looking at James with great determination to find the truth as James nods with an agreement.

"When are we going to visit that address?"

"Tonight," said James.

"Tonight! Why not ask permission from Professor Galdor and go during the daytime?" asked Henry worried.

"No—I don't want anyone else in the faculty to know about our doubt on Father Tolmen until we find out. Let's meet at the bell tower after the last bell for the day." Said, James.

"Count me in!" agreed Laura looking at the Davis brothers waiting for their response.

"Me too." Said Mathew and all three looking at Henry while his brother giving a sign for his word with a raise of an eyebrow.

"I prefer during the day but fine." Said Henry reluctantly and a face with slight fear.

The evening went as usual and dinner with all four without a word of their plan to sneak out in the middle of the night for a hunt of truth or to clear a doubt about Father Tolmen. The last bell rang to a melody for the students for a shut-eye to awake for a whole new day. As the bells ring the students scuttled into their congress quarters except for James, Laura, Henry, and Mathew. Hiding and walking through hallways in a way they are not noticed somehow got to the bell towers as planned. The little light drops on its dusty ceilings with cobwebs gave a mild light manageable to look around. James walked up to the window and opened it looking outside from the bell tower. He sees the massive knight guards on either side of each entrance door of the Phrontistery. Henry accidentally knocks on one of the bells as the clapper of the bell knocks on the metal making the silence slightly noisy.

"Shhh, Henry!" hushed Laura softly.

"Sorry" whispered Henry.

James quietly used his powers growing a climber plant into the bell tower through its window that was grown on a tree right after the Phrontistery bush fence. He grew the climber string to wrap around himself, Laura, Henry, and Mathew and uses his powers to carry them from the climber plant to take them down through the bell tower window to the ground. The spirit knight right next to them stands in position but fast asleep, and sleepily opens his eyes hearing the slight sound of steps as the four keep their feet on the ground. James, Laura, and Davis's brothers froze until the Spirit Knight falls back to sleep. James quietly steps forward-leaning to see if it's safe enough to run out to the tall Phrontistery fence. They jumped over the tall metal fence with Laura using her powers to grow four leaves of grass outside the fence and over it holding the leaf as a rope.

They ran through the quiet town which is usually busy and noisy hiding behind boards and stack stone walls avoiding the one or two-spirit pixies walking on the streets. The four walked through the pathway with fireflies flying all over the place. They sighted Gelda with Phanto like a scene of fairytale romance chatting and laughing under a tree, while Phanto puts a flower on Gelda's ear admiring her.

"Phanto and Gelda—who knew huh!" said Henry sarcastically in a soft voice. The two spirit pixies stood up walking towards the forest of trees that change the colors of the leaves are now dark and hardly visible to see the change of colors.

"Quick—hide!" said James as they all hid behind a large tree bark until they walked into the forest. The four quietly ran to Mose's house and peeped through the little window to look inside the tiny house.

 The house was lighted with two floating light drops on the ceiling, and Mose sleeping as he snores loudly on his little bed. The red pigeon was sleeping was tucking its head into its neck on the tree branch fixed on the wall.

"We got to get some sand but how can we get into the house?" asked Henry looking at the door on the locked with a thick metal chain and padlock through the edge of the window.

"The Chimney!" said James as he runs to the other side of the house with Laura and the Davis brothers following him. James using his Gravel powers grows a climber plant string that was grown not more than ten inches and grows wrapping around him as he did at the bell towers.

He goes through the narrow chimney to the fireplace by growing the climber plant string. There was burnt firewood but the fire was put out probably several hours ago. James walked out of the fireplace with chimney soot on his face, hands, and on the side of his green cape. He sees a clay pot on the ground in a corner of the room filled with glowing yellow sand. He slinked near the clay pot and takes a hand full of the glowing sand sneaking back into the fireplace wrapping the climber plant and taking him through the chimney and out of the little house. He slowly lands in front of Laura, Mathew, and Henry with a handful of glowing sand as he uses his power to get the climber plant stringer to its original size.

Is it enough for all four of us?" asked Mathew.

"Yes—let's get into pairs and throw the sand."

"What is the name of the place in the address?" asked Laura.

James took out the piece of paper saying "Watford Avenue." Henry and James paired up and Laura with Mathew as the four said "Watford Avenue raferogus" throwing the sand into their feet.

It was early morning as they all landed in between two walls that walk up to the road on the other side. Slightly cold weather, a dog barking, and a car drove fast with headlights as it is still close to daybreak. James takes out the piece of paper reading the address that says a house number "twenty-seven." They first walked past a residence numbered twenty on the post box, and passing the houses until they reached the right house.

"Well this is it I guess!" said James looking at the address on the piece of paper and the house. It was an old house but lively with flower pots hanging on the porch with two outdoor armchairs on the side.

James was about to walk up to the house and Laura stopped him from taking a step further.

"What is it? Asked James"

"Is it normal we just walk up to the house in robes and capes?"

"She's right! I tell you what—let's get to our parents house and change into some ordinary clothes and it's not too far." Said Mathew.

"But can we walk in wearing capes and robes to your house?" asked James.

"Of course—our parents are just like us and for them, the Pinnacle of Aries and the Phrontistery is just another normal life." Said, Henry.

"Let's take the bus!" suggested Mathew.

It was too early in the morning for the bus to be crowded and the only two people were the driver who seems to not care what they were wearing, most probably thinking its some hideous costume or a school play. They got up on the bus with Mathew tossing some coins, and the four walked up to the back seat. There was an old woman fast asleep leaning her head onto the window on the second seat on the left. They got off the bus and walked up to the house, and it is a bit brighter than before as they were close to sunrise.

The house was an average family house and nothing fancy, and an old car parked on the side front of the garage. They walked up to the front door ringing the bell, and after a few seconds, a dark brown hair lady with dark eyes and heavy in weight opened the door. She wore a printed dress that was long right after covering her knees and a pink bathrobe untied like an overcoat. Her hair was tied up and uncombed seems like she just woke up.

"Hi Mom," said Henry.

"Goodness boys! I must be dreaming." Said the lady as she looks at Laura and James slightly confused.

"Oh, mother—this is Laura and James our friends back at the Phrontistery.

"Oh come on in—but what brings you, children, here all of sudden it is not even the end of the term isn't it?"

"Oh we came here to help James to get some things—so we thought to come and see you." Said Henry as his mother was smiling and pleased to hear the thoughtfulness to drop by.

"By the way mother where is papa?" asked Mathew

"He is out of town for some research work for his lab—he did say that he would go to Aries after he returns to meet some of his old friends. So you children are in the same class as Henry and Mathew." Asked the Davis brother's mother looking at James and Laura giving a warm smile.

"Yes—I am Laura Wilson," said Laura as she handshake introducing herself.

"James Spinner—a pleasure to meet you, Mrs. Davis," said James as he reached out his hand for a handshake. Mrs. Davis kept both hands crossed on the chest fully shocked and surprised with eyes wide looking at James from head to toe without a handshake. She grabbed his face and looked closely and hugged him so tight that made breathing a difficult task for James a tight hug.

"Oh James—you are really him—Johanna's son!" said Mrs. Davis in excitement.

"You knew my mother?"

Of course—I have not closely associated her but there is hardly anyone who does not know her. They were plenty who looked up to that great lady. I am so glad you are all in the same class—anyway my name's Martha Payne—Davis my maiden name of course."

"Mother we need some clothes—we cannot travel anywhere around here with robes and capes." Said Mathew.

"Certainly! Well, I can talk to Mrs. Ashwood who lives two blocks away—she tailors clothes for two or three small clothing boutiques in town."

"But we can't stay for long mom—will she be up at this hour?"

"Oh, no doubt about that! A lark she is— gets up at the crack of Dawn. Let me see what I can do. You children make yourselves at home." Said Mrs. Davis as she walked out of the door closing it behind her.

Mathew and Henry went upstairs to change and James looked around the house. There was an upright piano with photos of Henry and Mathew when they were very young. A black and white little framed photograph of Mr. and Mrs. Davis's wedding portrait and a photograph of two men with Mr. and Mrs. Davis wearing robes. A picture probably takes at the Pinnacle of Aries and seems ideally a normal happy blessed to be a part of the world of Aries. Mrs. Davis walked in with some clothes and handed them over to James and Laura.

"Here you go children—these were to deliver next week she gave me for half the price of what to be tagged in the retail store."

"Thank you, Mrs. Davis—it's very kind of you." Said Laura as Henry walked downstairs with a change of clothes.

"You are most welcome. Pumpkin can you take them upstairs to change." Said Mrs. Davis making Henry embarrassed for the pet name said in front of his friends. They walked upstairs and Henry gave his room to Laura and Mathew gave his to James.

All four walked downstairs and walked out of the door with Mrs. Davis following them.

"You children take care of yourselves—will see you all soon at the term-end. Oh, wait! Do you children have enough glowing sand to go back to Aries" asked Mrs. Davis?

"Actually we didn't think about that—we don't have any left mom!" said Henry.

"I am glad you all dropped by—always remember to have glowing sand if you step out of Aries at any given time." Said Mrs. Davis as she was caring and a typical mother hen giving a small bottle filled with glowing sand to Mathew.

"This will be enough for all four of you to use for about two times. Once you get to Mose he will give you sand to leave from there."

"You mean we cannot get to the Phrontistery directly?" asked James confused

"Of course not dear—that will be unsafe if anyone can enter the Pinnacle of Aries as they wish—won't it? Only the faculty management can go or leave as they please to go anywhere without landing on the gatekeeper's premises. He appears the door when you are required if not—to the gatekeeper's premises then to the land of Aries—but only till you get your own power stones"

"Thank you, Mrs. Davis." Said James as they left and Henry was reluctant to leave as she turned around after walking halfway in their lawn waving at his mother.

"Oh no—we have to sneak in again!" said Henry and Mathew hit his arm with a pat on his elbow to avoid being caught that they are here without permission from the faculty.

"What did you say?" asked Mrs. Davis

"Come on Pumpkin—we got to go finish this soon and get back to the Phrontistery." Said James sarcastically as Mathew and Laura both laughed.

"Very funny James!" said Henry slightly responding sarcastically back at the teasing,

They were finally in ordinary clothes worn in the human world and front of the house as mentioned in the address. They rang the bell door and a man opened the door looking at the faces of James, Laura, and Davis brothers confusedly. James recognized the man as the person who was speaking to his aunt about selling the house James's mother lived in. The man did not recognize James since he had never seen or spoken to James personally. Except for the fact he was aware, a boy lived with Mr. and Mrs. Walsh, and now with the incorrect statement that he was adopted out of the family.

"Good morning—apologies to trouble you this early—we are here to meet someone for an urgent matter sir?" said Mathew.

"Who is it that you wish to speak to?" asked the man.

"Father Tolmen is he here?" asked Laura.

"I met him yesterday and he brought a property closing a deal—a great one I should say!"

"Where about Mister…?"

"Carter—what is your need to know may I ask? The property owned by him and I cannot disclose much about any of my client's personal details—I hope you children understand."

"Yes, Mr. Carter—we apologize we didn't mean to trouble you. We were said to come to the place to start on the research work we were set to do—I believe Father Tolmen came to find a place for it. He gave us your address before he left." said Mathew.

"Why didn't you children say that before? It's Number fourteen at Wimbly Hills Residencies down the street and turn left. It's not difficult to find!"

James was shocked to hear the address and the precise location of the place he lived in his childhood with his mother, and also the place he rightfully owns.

"Thank you, Mr. Carter! By the way, will Father Tolmen visit you again?" asked Laura.

"There is no reason to—but there are some paper he has to send me—he mentioned he will send it by post. Why are you asking anyway?"

"Oh, no reason at all Mr. Carter—you seem like a nice person, thank you for your help." Said Laura and it was visible that Mr. Carter was pleased with the compliment.

"It's my pleasure—good luck with finding the place for your research.

"Thank you, Mr. Carter, "said Henry.

The man closed the door, and the four stepped down the stairs of the porch as they now got to proceed with finding the place travelling back to the painful yet sweet past of James.

"Let's take the train it's easier!" said Henry. They went to the station and got into a train sitting on one of the red two leather seats two on each.

"James what is it?" asked Laura looking at James as he looked disappointed and hurt.

"That address—it is my mother's house. Mr. Carter was the man my aunt was speaking to about my mother's house"

Laura, Mathew, and Henry looked at each other fully shocked as they hardly expected it to be their friend's house that rightfully belongs to him.

"This is unbelievable—so the deal was brought to Mr. Carter by your aunt—but does that mean the Phrontistery know the owner of the house belongs to Mrs. Spinner?" Asked Mathew.

"I am sure the faculty trust him enough to not go in search of the history of the house. Besides according to Mr. Carter Father Tolmen is one who had brought the house." Said Laura.

"I can't believe it—so that is why he had my mother's death certificate."

"We still don't know why he purchased it James—it could be to avoid from losing your mother's house forever if an outsider buys it, and might be to give it back to you as you come of age." Said Mathew.

"Let's go find out—we didn't come all the way for nothing." Said, Henry. The train passed the breath-taking surroundings of mountains and trees with a slight mist and morning dew.

Chapter Eleven: Wimbly Hills Residencies

The journey feels stronger to James's mind from a trip to finding the most awaited truth to pain and emotions with a sweet memory of his mother alive and healthy. The surroundings seem familiar as it gets closer to the place. The station arrived as they got down and walked past the town to a path with trees on the sides.

"I have sweet memories walking down this narrow road—I used to walk with my mother in the evenings. We used to collect different types of rocks for my rocks collection."

"Did you remember your aunt visiting your mother often?" asked Laura.

"No—I remember Ciara's christening—I went with my mother and from that day onwards I only saw her when she came to pick me up after my mother passed away. I was told she had to do some tests at the hospital and I will have to stay with my aunt."

"Who told you that?" asked Henry

"The priest did," said James and the next few steps were much slower as he was lost in deep thought.

"What is it James?" asked Laura

"The priest—I do not remember clearly but I recall a face that looks …."

"Looks like who James?" asked Henry

"Father Tolmen!"

"You got to be kidding—are you sure?" asked Mathew concernedly.

"No I cannot confirm it exactly but finding the false death certificate at his chambers makes things more suspicious with the face I remember."

"Let's get to the house first." Said Laura.

They came to a narrow road with a wooden board fixed on the ground that says "Wimbly Hills Residencies". Walking down its sandy path as it leads to an old two-story house that is quite massive. James stopped as he felt a strong sense of painful emotions running through him as he stops front of the half-opened gates.

"Are you alright?" asked Henry from James concernedly.

"Yes!"

They stepped into the premises of the lawn that had some bushes dried and surely was abandoned and uncleaned for years. It was nothing inviting with stepping to the dry lawn and all four were suddenly thrown backward by some strong unseen force. They fell on their backs and were completely shocked by the unexpected power that avoided them from entering the land.

"That's not a nice welcome!" Said Henry sarcastically as he dusted his back.

"What is that?" asked James in shock.

"It's protected from anyone entering—but this can't be by Father Tolmen!" Said Laura curiously.

"What do you mean?" asked Mathew.

"Father Tolmen is in Adam's Ale isn't it?" asked Laura looking at Mathew and Henry

"Yes..." replied Mathew curiously.

"Restriction of entering a land is a mastery skill with a resourceful power stone by just two congresses. It is either by Gravel or Welkin—and usually, the attacking force by air is done by Welkin, and if it's a Gravel source power it is a force to push the intruders away with a movement of the ground."

"So which means this is by a Welkin's power." said Henry.

"I don't think so—look!" said James as he pointed to the ground of the entrance. There was a speck of black dust mixed into the sand that divides the road and entrance to the land.

"Careful don't go too near it," said Henry.

"Seems like not any kind of source power." Said Laura.

"What does that mean?" asked Mathew.

"Witchcraft!" said Laura taking the attention of all three at her unexpected response.

"Are you sure?" asked James.

James saw two people from a distance walking towards the house, and one is Father Tolmen and the other is a man wearing a suit with a black trench coat.

"Quick hide!" said James as they all hid behind the trees in the woods behind them. The tree trunks were broad for a great cover to hide. James, Laura, and Davis's brother's peeps watching carefully as the two men were approaching the gates. The man not once turns towards them to recognize the face or to have a slight notice of his face.

"Who is that with Father Tolmen?" asked Henry.

They stopped a few steps back avoiding walking into the power restricting them to enter the land. It seems like they were very much aware of where the power throws back the one that steps in.

"What are they going to do?" asked Laura as they were watching the two men facing the house.

The man with Father Tolmen took out a power stone and after a few seconds, the sand that mixed with the black dust and a cloud of black smoke was absorbed to power stone.

"Do you guys see what I'm seeing?" asked Henry as they were looking with eyelids raised to the highest staring with wide eyes.

The two men walked into the premises without any barrier and walked into the house.

"Let's go!" said James and Laura stopped him holding from his arm.

"No" cried out Laura.

"Why not? We got to find what he is up to."

"James I understand that you want to find everything the soonest since this matter means a lot to you—but remember we got to do this without getting ourselves in trouble." Said Mathew.

"Besides we don't know if there is any danger just we four can fight!" said Laura looking curiously at the house.

"If we go back we've come here for nothing!" Said James looking at his friends with great confidence in his eyes.

James stepped out of the woods and the three followed him as they walked towards the gate. The power of the mysterious man's power stone did not take away the power of anyone to enter. They were thrown back the same way as before as they fell on their backs.

"One thing is for sure—we are going to go back to the Phrontistery with a bad back," said Mathew as he stretched holding his hips.

"The power is restored—we cannot enter through the gates," said Henry.

"What are we going to do?" asked Laura.

Father Tolmen walked outside and closed the gates fully taking out the board fixed at the middle of the lawn that says "for sale" and walked back inside.

"It's Father Tolmen," said Mathew and the four soon hid again behind the fully grown trees at the woods to avoid Father Tolmen seeing them as they couldn't hide anywhere close to the walls with the power restricting them to come near the premises. The only thought all four were in is to find a way to get inside the house avoiding coming in contact with the power that covers for protection.

James noticed a troop of ants walking down the tree bark he was hiding towards the ground and it seems like it goes out of the woods to the other side of the sandy path. After Father Tolmen goes back into the house, James stepped out on the walking path following the colony of ants.

"Where are you going James?" asked Mathew as they followed him.

"I wonder where these ants are going."

The ants go around the front wall and through a small hole at the bottom with a crack on the wall at the side without any interruption. The grass is dry and brown and bushes next to the front wall are wilted with the dirt on the ground mixed with black dust. The grass outside grown in the middle of the sidewall is healthy and green.

"If the power restricts not even an insect could enter." Said Laura.

James walked up to the edge of the wall and reached out to touch doubtfully not knowing if he would be thrown back. His palm reached the wall and felt the bricks on the wall without any force undoing his presence near the premises.

"Let's get inside from here." Said, James.

"You go first James," said Mathew as he gathered his hands with Henry to give him a push to reach the top of the wall. James was lifted and he grabbed the top of the wall putting his legs and jumped to the garden.

"You next Laura!" said Henry as she was lifted and James helped her jump to the ground from the other side. Likewise, Mathew helped his younger brother and once everyone is on the other side he jumped up putting a foot on the middle of the wall to give himself a push to reach the top of the wall. It was not too difficult with his height for a quick jump over the old English garden wall.

They ran into the house covering themselves through the dried bushes and slightly bowing down to avoid anyone seeing them from inside the house.

"Quick this way!" said James taking them around his childhood home. There was a window shut and James manage to open it.

"This is the maid's bedroom—no one would have a purpose to walk into this room unless someone uses it."

"What if someone does?" asked Henry whispering.

"No—all the furniture in the room is still covered with sheets."

They got into the house through the little window without making a noise. They walked up to the door and James touched the doorknob slowly turning it open. The man's and Father Tolmen's voices were heard as it got closer. The maid's room was near the entrance and as the two men walked from inside the house to the entrance door the voices became much clearer. The lights in the hall comes through the small gap between the floor and the wooden door of the maid's bedroom. The shadows of the two men is visible and moves in the light that peaks between the floor and the wooden door as they pass the maid's bedroom walking up to the main entrance of the house as they speak pausing a few steps away from the door.

"It was a close one to get this deal—the whole blabber of Carter about the papers is getting under my skin." Said the man. James, Laura, Mathew, and Davis do the eavesdropping behind the maid's bedroom door.

"I will take care of that!" said Father Tolmen.

"The proof—did you find it?" asked the man.

"Not yet! But it's just a matter of withholding the truth from sight. We need to get the power stones soon and Professor Galdor will allocate staff to this matter which will make our task much easier. Make sure he wouldn't get the slightest doubt about our purpose of finding any of this!"

"We shouldn't let Rebecca on the loose too." Said the man.

"No—she would be nothing but helpless, the only problem is her power stone is at the Phrontistery."

"That boy is crossing his lines—that Spinner! Finish him first before anything else."

"Yes!" replied Father Tolmen.

James, Laura, and the Davis brothers were taken by surprise listening to the conversation between the two men standing behind the door the four was listening.

"Father Tolmen! He is involved with the Witchcrafts?" whispered Mathew looking at James and Laura making a line between his dark eyebrows.

Father Tolmen went back into the house after the man left, and it was the perfect timing for the four to sneak out of the maid's bedroom. They ran through the hall that had furniture covered in white sheets, a red dusty rug on the floor with wall-mounted lampshades on the sides of the walls, and the rich crafted crystal glass chandelier lighting up the hall. The four ran upstairs and sneaked into each room cautiously to observe. The master bedroom had the bed uncovered that flows memories to James of his mother lying unconsciously. There was a beautiful painting on the wall right above the bed of a mermaid. When James was younger he just saw it as an artistic and beautiful painting of a mermaid in a breath-taking surrounding painted by Mrs. Johanna Spinner herself. James is now a young boy aware of things he never thought could exist like the Pinnacle of Aries that made him recognize the painting was not just some mermaid but a painting of Esther, the queen of lotus.

They walked downstairs walking through the hallway passing the kitchen of a cozy interior with hardwood kitchen cupboards, and two rooms with one tightly closed door. One of the rooms was locked and the other had a pencil-thin gap between the door and the door frame that showed a dim light behind the door. James slowly pushed the door opening to a gap to see the room. There were candles fixed in wax all over the floor, and a symbol was drawn on the wooden floor planks of a large star drawn in the middle of the room with a circle around it. Father Tolmen was sitting on the floor right in the middle of the symbol facing the window like in deep meditation. The window was covered with a thick maroon color faded cloth.

"It looks some kind of a ritual!" whispered Henry.

Father Tolmen raised his hands holding a power stone with a black beaded chain attached to it.

"Death beads!" said Laura.

"What?" James whispered asking confusedly and the Davis brother's waiting to hear what it is all about.

"The death beads are used in witchcrafts plucked in the garden of souls. It is the garden that buries the witches and their souls exist with powers of the after-death."

"This means Father Tolmen is with the witchcrafts!" said Mathew

"That also mean—he-he is—he is helping Burton." Said Henry whispering in fear with a face about to cry.

"Hello James," said Father Tolmen behind them. The four startled and looked around and it was Father Tolmen standing with that calm and pleasant smile as usual. James looked back at the room and Father Tolmen was seated doing the ritual but he was also standing right in front of them.

"This is impossible!" said James.

"Oh, you don't know about the real essence of powers yet James. I will tell you what—you join me and I will train you to be the greatest enchanter even better than your mother."

"No! The Phrontistery is the place that creates the greatest enchanters—and I do not wish to do anything harmful with my source powers."

"Harmfulness is a defense mechanism, James. It is a source of intelligence!"

"Wrong! How can you be this selfish?"

"If you have powered it is difficult to survive being sensitive James!"

"Who are you really?" asked Mathew.

"I am no different—a spirit guide indeed, but a one with a greater insight about life, power, greatness, and much—much more."

"You will regret this—all of this!" shouted Laura.

"Let's go." Shouted James as he ran away with the others following him and runs downstairs. As they were about to enter the maid's bedroom downstairs the door shuts on its own with a strong bang.

Father Tolmen walked downstairs calmly and looks at them smiling but a sense of a strained smile is felt strongly to James.

"There is no point of running from here. Please make yourselves at home and you are my guests." Said Father Tolmen calmly.

"This house belongs to me!" shouted James with a wave of unbearable anger.

"How is it you are going to prove it, James? Anything in this human world is very limited—especially the little thing called proof. You are the only son of the famous enchantress Johanna Spinner—but how is it accepted here may I ask? You are dead to the human world but the most important future enchanter alive to the Pinnacle of Aries.

Tie them up!" shouted Father Tolmen after his calm explanation of lies and betrayal to the faculty, James, and the entire Pinnacle of Aries turning his calmness to an evil look in his eyes. Four witches emerged through the walls and one from the floor. They wore ragged robes with white hair long up to their toes, and their pale faces and hands that seemingly has no drop of blood in them. The witches grabbed Laura, Davis brothers and James. Henry and Mathew with the hands cold as ice bringing the witch bodies to life with dark spells and power of Johanna Spinner's power stone. They dragged them effortlessly into the storeroom underneath the stairs with incredible strength while the James, Laura and Davis brother were trying to get themselves loose from the tight hold of the witches.

"A door locked with a spell can never be opened even by the strength of the strongest man or tool in the world," said one of the witches with an evil chuckle as she shut the door making the loudest bang a small wooden door could make.

"We got to get out of here!" cried out Laura.

"Quick the sand!" said James looking at Mathew.

He took the tiny bottle of sand his mother gave and poured some to the palms of his brother, Laura, and James.

"Aries raferogus," said all four as they threw the sand to their feet.

They appeared right in front of Mose's house, and the most unexpected and worse appearing was to end up being right in front of the midget man feeding peanuts to his pigeon.

"You—how dare you all! Do you know the worries you've all caused in the faculty and us in the great land of Aries eh! Obviously when we who have better things to worry about—and here you are just wander about like a bunch of witless weasels?"

"We are sorry Mose—we had to go because…" said James and Mose interrupted before he could complete the explanation for leaving without informing.

"I do not wish to hear all that jabber eh—explain to Professor Galdor, and he is very disappointed in you—all of you!" said Mose frowning and displeased as he grabbed James's and Henry's arms taking them to the faculty with Laura and Mathew following them.

They passed the spirit knights besides the gates and walked through the lobby with the limestone moving statues on the sides, and reception elves looking at them curiously and some surprised. The faculty seems to be aware of their disappearance and two girls walked passed looking at them as they whispered something to each other with their hands hugging the books into their chests. They walked up to Professor Galdor's office knocking on the door, and almost instantly Professor Galdor's voice was heard to come in. Mose reached the doorknob above his head and turned to open the door. Professor Galdor looked up, and he sighted Henry fully dreaded, his brother Mathew hiding his fear courageously like James and Laura. The moment the four were seen by Professor Galdor his calmed face turned to anger, and he looked at them closely over his glasses slightly bowing down his head. He stood up from his majestic-looking high back chair, and Mose finally stepped into the office room holding James and Henry's arms with Laura and Mathew walking behind them.

"Pardon me if disturbed sir—to my bewilderment these trouble-makers appeared in my cottage land plot. I fervently believe they've taken some sand and left the Pinnacle of Aries without my knowledge and definitely without the faculty's consent."

"Yes they sure have—thank you, Mose. Please inform Professor Cuppins to call off the search party and that the arrival of the four students." Said Professor Galdor.

Mose slightly bowed in respect and wobbled back out the office room closing the door behind him.

"Care to explain your unacceptable vanishing from the Pinnacle breaking countless rules of the faculty?" asked Professor Galdor as he walked around the table and stood in front of them.

"We are so sorry Professor—please forgive us. Please Professor Galdor!" said Henry with a voice stammering with fear and eyes of worry.

"Please sir—forgive them! It was my idea, and I am the one responsible." Said James with Professor Galdor turned from Henry to James.

"It is a great thing to be direct and honest James—but may I ask what made you do such a thing of beyond the pale taking your friends with you? We even have a search party by forces looking for all of you almost everywhere in the Pinnacle of Aries" said Professor Galdor looking at James curiously.

"Sir—Father Tolmen—he is nothing like any of us sir?"

"What are you talking about boy?"

"He is with the witchcrafts?" said James. Professor Galdor remained silent and confused looking at James.

"When you asked about Father Tolmen the other day—was with it because you doubted he is with the evil?"

 "No sir—we wanted to know the truth. The address he gave was the realtor to buy the place for the matter of the Phrontistery to protect the power stones in the human world. But—but he-he."

"What is it, James?"

"Sir—he had got a place for the purpose, but for the side of the evil. He uses dark spells and witchcraft. He locked us up with the help of the witches blocking us with the dark powers, but we escaped with the glowing sand appearing right in front of Mose."

"Yes sir—please believe us! Father Tolmen had a power stone with death beads. We saw it for our own eyes." Said Laura stepping forward with eyes that looked disturbed.

"We got to go back and stop him if not all the power stones will go to Burton."

Professor Galdor took a deep breath and exhaled and looked at the four carefully.

"I believe you, James and the rest of you—let me have a talk to Professor Sisko and Professor Cuppins about this, and let's do whatever it takes after the management confirms these facts as accurate enough to proceed. Until then do not talk about this to anyone especially your fellow students no matter how much trust and fellowship you may have. This is no simple matter and I hope that you all understand— we will have to take this matter with the management very seriously."

"Yes sir! Said, James.

"Now—as to all of you I have to say that this is reasonable to leave in your perspective, but you should have taken permission. I am surprised you didn't even speak to me in this regard before you do such an unconscionable act ignoring the faculty rules. I am afraid that you will have a yearly reduction of your overall scores to your report books."

Laura and Henry looked fully disappointed since scores in academics and overall performance means so much to them than James or Mathew.

"Sir—pardon me for asking this—but you mentioned you have to confirm these facts are true and accurate to proceed—is there any doubt on what we say to you sir?" asked Mathew curiously yet humbly.

"No Mr. Davis—I believe what you all say, but what I believe and not believe will not matter to the faculty processors and management. There are faculty protocols that concern the Bureau of Education since it involves a strong accusation of one of the Phrontistery management party.

"Yes sir—we understand." Said Mathew.

They walked to their quarters as Laura and James walked into the Gravel quarters taking the attention of all the students in the faculty as they walked through the dorm.

"Where were you off to?" asked one of the boys from James.

James was almost to respond and Professor Cuppins rushed into the quarters calling out his name excited and worried.

"James! Goodness where were you, and you with those three always up to somewhere once being caught to Professor Lansford all soaking wet and now disappeared for nearly a day!" said Professor Cuppins looking at James concernedly.

"We are fine Professor Cuppins." Replied James calmly.

"This is the first and the last time you step out of the Pinnacle of Aries without prior approval—do you understand?"

"Yes Professor Cuppins." Replied James as she left off walking through the boy's quarter dorm to the girl's quarters.

When everyone was asleep James walked to his door of the room of his belongings and the narrow bathroom quietly.

"Master I need to speak to you!" said James closing his eyes and after a few seconds he heard the rattle sound opening his eyes of a pigeon. He was in the dark cave with the spirit dragon with red pigeons sleeping all over the cave as one or two flaps its wings to make its tiny zone of comfort.

 "Master!"

"How are you, young enchanter? That's a great think to go in search for what you believe!"

"I am fine Master—I need your help. I need to know what I should do. I cannot put myself and my friends in trouble by sneaking out to undo what Father Tolmen is up to, at the same time I cannot just wait without doing nothing too."

"James! If there is something that stops you from doing what you intended to do—you find a way in that problem itself first."

"How can I do that master?"

"What is it you really want to do James?" asked the spirit dragon looking at James graciously.

"I want to stop Father Tolmen Master! We cannot let Burton get his hands on those Power Stones."

"What stops you from doing that?"

"The Phrontistery master!"

"Then you have to find a way through the Phrontistery to do what you need to do!" replied the Spirit Dragon calmly. James thought for some time and expressed excitement with an idea.

"Yes! That's it—I can go back with the faculty management's support. But what if they refuse?"

"There is always a way James—a word, a resource, a plan, a proof. You just need to find the right one." Said the Spirit Dragon and James suddenly appeared to be back facing the mirror on the wall of his quarter room.

"Good morning Mathew!" said Laura as she was walking through the hallways with James to the dining room and Mathew joining them.

"Where is Henry?" asked Laura.

"Oh, he woke up late—I just noticed he was snoring and fast asleep in his pajamas when I was about to walk out of the quarters. I woke him up and not a single one was still sleeping then. Seems like the loud bells didn't bother the tiredness of a night's lack of sleep." Said Mathew sarcastically.

"What are we going to do now James?" asked Mathew with Laura turning towards James curiously.

"We go back—but not alone this time!" said James.

"What do you mean?" asked Laura

"We will need Professor Galdor and the faculty's support. We can't do this on our own—but there is a possibility the faculty management would not agree."

"Are you going to speak to Professor Galdor about it?"

"Yes! We have to find a way—one way or another!" said James with confidence. Henry came running behind them and catches up to them.

"Sorry I'm late—I overslept!"

"Before we do anything—let's go get some breakfast first! I could eat a horse having to go through all that without rest or food." Replied Mathew.

The morning went as usual and lecture sessions with not an hour away from the day's schedule. James awaits to speak to Professor Galdor at a time convenient, and the classes were done by substitute student supporters in the post-graduate faculty since Professor Galdor is in a serious staff discussion about the matter which James, Laura, and the two Davis brothers brought to him yesterday in the late evening.

Chapter Twelve: Evidence of Truth

The usual morning turned to afternoon and finally, Professor Sisko walked into the room after a lengthy staff discussion. The students were wondering and some engaging in the conversations on what the matter was for all the lecturers and management to be in such a long discussion during lecture hours. It was only aware by James, Laura, Henry, and Mathew, but as they were told by Professor Galdor everything remained confidential among the four without a word uttered or even to be guessed by any of the fellow students.

"Thank you Travis!" said Professor Sisko as he released the post-graduate student from his class.

Professor Sisko took over the class and looked around calmly.

"Alright, we have an hour left. Turn to page—one hundred and fourteen in your textbooks." Said Professor Sisko as he walks through the class.

The bells rang and it was the end of the lecture session for morning hours, and students picked up their books from the table and walked out of the classroom door.

"James a quick word please—you too Miss Wilson and the Davises," said Professor Sisko."

James, Laura, and the Davis brother remained in the class waiting until all the students have left.

Professor Sisko leaned on the lecturer's desk while the four walked up to, and they confirmedly knew it was about the matter spoken to the faculty principal about Father Tolmen.

"How are you all? Is everyone alright?" asked Professor Sisko looking concerned at them.

"Yes, Professor Sisko." Replied James.

"I was flabbergasted to know what you all have discovered—especially about Father Tolmen. I do hope you understand how dangerous it is to be in contact with these matters on your own."

"Yes Professor Sisko—but honestly we did not have the slightest doubt that Father Tolmen is with the witchcrafts." Said Mathew.

"Yes Professor Sisko not even a doubt—of course we did suspect he was up to something but not to this extent." Said Laura raising her eyebrows with surprise as she speaks.

"I can't blame you! It was clear least one was not in shock when Professor Galdor addressed it."

"Well, to be honest with you—I had the same thought during the meeting."

"What is that Professor?" asked James curiously.

"Father Tolmen joined the Phrontistery about three years ago—Father Lukas was the one before him. Great man indeed—but died with the old age. He was here almost for forty years, and even when I was a young enchanter—and oh how I dreamt of graduating with my power stone. Father Tolmen was in his later years was sent to us by the Bureau after Father Lukas passed away, but this is also his first time to work in a faculty or any kind of an organization."

"Where was he before?" asked Mathew with a glance at James.

"We were informed that Father Tolmen is a spirit guide who worked on his own and helped many, but only till he was about thirty-two years of age. After that, he was not here—at the Pinnacle of Aries."

"Then—where was he, Professor? Asked Laura curiously.

"In the human world of course—living completely detached to the Pinnacle of Aries in just a most ordinary human life." Said Professor Sisko calmly.

"Which means he never used his powers or his power stone till he came back?" asked James astound.

"That's right!"

James strongly knew the best person to trust after Professor Galdor is none other than Professor Sisko, a man with genuine intentions, empathy, and no skullduggery. There is only one way left to achieve anything close to fully stopping Father Tolmen is by going back to his childhood home. The way left to convince the management, even if Professor Galdor agrees to take students who are yet to graduate not even close to having their power stone is through Professor Sisko. It was clear to James and his friends that the faculty management cannot take an independent decision on this matter but with the approval of the Bureau.

"Professor Sisko—we need to go back and stop Father Tolmen." Said, James

"Yes Professor you have to help us!" said Laura pleasingly.

"Of course—but May I ask you what triggered you to go in search of Father Tolmen?"

James, Laura, Henry, and Mathew looked at each other worriedly while Professor Sisko looks at them fully curious narrowing his eyes.

"Professor Sisko—you are the first to know about this!"

"What is it, James?"

"We found my mother's death certificate at Father Tolmen's chambers—it was a reliable nor true but with a great lie saying she died with cancer. It was the reason why we went to the human world without faculty's knowledge." Said James and Professor Sisko thought about it for some seconds and nodded.

"I understand—I will help you. Before anything you need to speak to Professor Galdor about this."

"Yes, Professor Sisko—I will speak to him in the evening today itself!"

The evening sessions started and ended as the bells rang for the day's lectures to be over. James rushed to Professor Galdor's chambers to speak about handling this which is now more than just a concern that should be directed based on a formal decision to remove Father Tolmen from the Phrontistery but involves deeply to James as a personal matter. It meant so much more to him every ounce of justice to himself and the Pinnacle of Aries. He stood in front of Professor Galdor's chambers taking a deep breath and exhaled to calm his nervousness feeling.

He unexpectedly heard Professor Galdor's voice behind him, and as he turned around as he sees Professor Galdor walking towards his chambers looking at James calmly.

"James! Are you here to see me?"

"Yes sir."

Professor Galdor opened the door allowing James to walk into his chambers with a simple office desk on the side with a wooden chair and a bed on the other side.

"I addressed the matter with the management in the morning and to the Bureau—it was quite a challenge to convince the disturbing information without disclosing the fact that a few undergraduate students found out by traveling to the human world without our permission. It will come to a different concern if we say we allow undergraduates to traverse such risky things without supervision and care of the management. However, the Bureau look into this starting with a background check of Father Tolmen more in-depth and let us know—probably within this week."

"To tell you frankly Professor Galdor there is no time to wait—there were witches that trapped us and luckily we had glowing sand to escape. There was another man with Father Tolmen too."

"Who was that James—did you recognize him?"

"No! But he seems to be aware of everything—about buying the place from Mr. Carter, the realtor and taking the power stones—he even spoke about my aunt with Father Tolmen."

"Your aunt! What did you hear him say?"

"Father Tolmen told him that my aunt's power stone is at the Phrontistery—and—and..." James looked down in disappointment.

"What is it, boy?"

"I feel she is also in danger sir." Said James looking with worrisome eyes.

"I understand what you are feeling—but unfortunately as the management of the Phrontistery especially myself, this is out of our hands James. Mainly because it involves an accusation to one of the Phrontistery management and academic professional. Something very unlikely for a faculty management personal could receive."

"But sir—I"

"I understand James that you are worried about your aunt, and also you fight for what is right courageously. No offense James—but to take it over completely to our hands, and involve you—neither you nor your friends qualify to provide a good reason to why any undergraduate students involved in such a menacing matter willingly. Even if we are born with the born blessings of the Spirit Dragon—we got nothing to say if they question your involvement."

"Sir my aunt is in danger and I got to go back home..." Professor Galdor barged in questioning confusedly.

"Home? What do you mean you got to go back home?"

James finally took some great sense of courage to tell everything to Professor Galdor despite not knowing if he could react adversely than to understand even though Professor Galdor said he trust them.

"What are you trying to tell me, dear boy?"

"Sir—for quite some time we doubted Father Tolmen. On the day Laura was attacked—we heard Burton's voice but it was Father Tolmen in the bell tower."

Professor remained silent listening to James carefully as he narrows his eyes with a penetrating stare at James.

"My doubt is why—why would Father Tolmen show he is involved with Burton so openly?" asked Professor Galdor curiously.

"We were led by showing signs to go up to the bell tower—signs with spirit feathers that's glowing and red that showed the way. I thought those were signs by the Spirit Dragon the little did we knew it was a trap led by Father Tolmen to satisfy Burton's wish and attacked Laura. It sure was the perfect way to find where my aunt is and her power stone. Secondly, we sneaked to Father Tolmen's chambers, and we found my mother's death certificate sent to him. The details on it were not even true—it said that my mother died of cancer. That made Father Tolmen even more suspicious because it was absurd that a person in the faculty management need some false death certificate knowing the dark truth. Thirdly, the day after the attack to the Phrontistery Father Tolmen was missing and we were told that he is away for a couple of days."

"Was it then you came to see me inquire about where Father Tolmen is?"

"Yes sir—the address you gave me is a person named Mr. Carter, who was the realtor my aunt spoke about selling the property that belonged to my mother. It was the same person I saw back at my aunt's house. When we went to the address Father Tolmen had given you, and that was when we were told that Father Tolmen had purchased a place which is called "Wimbly Hills Residencies." It—it—it was…"

Professor Galdor held James's shoulder and encouraging him to speak.

"What is it James—this place—does it belong to your mother?" asked Professor Galdor and James trying to finally control his emotions to speak, and he succeeded.

"Sir—I heard my aunt speaking to Mr. Carter, and I heard there is some sort of a Trust Will to the house which states after my mother's passing I will have the rights to the house—I am not very much aware of what the Trust Will do sir. My aunt lied to the realtor saying I died in an accident, and when he inquired her about the boy living with her she said I was only adopted to overcome the pain of her nephew's death."

Professor Galdor's curiosity turned to anger as he looked up furious lost in some thought.

"It was my childhood home sir—I lived there with my mother until I was taken by my aunt."

Professor Galdor's anger turned to sadness as he looked down at James.

"I don't know how—but it is important in every way to stop Father Tolmen. Please sir I need to go back!"

"I understand dear boy, and I will take this to the Bureau personally to take approval for you to go under faculty permission. I will have to speak about this with Professor Cuppins as well." Professor Galdor took a deep breath looking at James curiously.

"I do need to ask you something."

"What is that sir?"

"You mentioned that your aunt told Mr. Carter that you were adopted—are you sure if that is what was said rigorously?"

"Yes sir! I am positive!"

"James you and I have to go on a small trip, but before that, there are few things I will have to take care of. I think we have a great piece of proof to get your involvement and stop whatever that is about to happen at that house."

"Thank you, sir." Said James as he left Professor Galdor's chambers. James had a slight smile and feeling of satisfaction about Professor Galdor being involved to help him save the danger to Pinnacle of Aries, and as well as the house filled with his childhood memories and his mother.

It was a great relief for James having to open up to Professor Galdor that was burning within him having to prove his reasons in wanting to find the truth by breaking faculty rules. Laura and the Davis brothers walked towards him from the opposite direction through the hallway passing the Gravel wall on one side, and the stone wall on the side as the shadows of a loft of pigeons flying across the walls with its shrill whistle of the wings and soft pigeon calls.

"James—did you speak to Professor Galdor?" asked Laura

"Yes, and he agreed to speak to the Bureau and give authority for me to go back with the permission and help of the faculty."

"That great James!" said Mathew excitedly.

"Which mean you told everything?"

"Yes… Everything!."

Late in the evening, the seriousness of the matter was undoubtedly running in Professor Galdor's mind. Professor Galdor hastily walking back and forth in the meeting room looking worried and unsettled. Professor Cuppins seated in one of the chairs with her fingers pressed against her narrow lips looking slightly disturbed and wondering about a serious matter.

"I can't believe it—that poor boy! How much he need to bear all of this?" said Professor Cuppins taking looking at the faculty president.

"It is very difficult indeed—but I must say that James has some great inner strength just like Johanna. I am truly glad to see the personalities of these young future enchanters."

"Yes definitely. What shall we do about this Professor Galdor?"

"There is one way to get some solid proof for the Bureau to accept our permission and guidance for James to engage in this matter."

"What is that?"

"Ms. Rebecca Spinner's lie on her nephew's passing—we need to speak to the person who made the deal with Father Tolmen. Also, I was told there is a Trust Will by Johanna to the house"

"Mr. Carter?"

"Yes."

"I cannot imagine how she could do this to her own sister's child."

"Well—we all know about Rebecca! She will do anything to keep herself and anything that has to do with her from Burton."

"I will do a visit to speak to Mr. Carter tomorrow—first thing in the morning." Said Professor Cuppins and uttered with great determination.

It was early morning and a start of a day cold with the morning dew drips down the faculty window glasses as the day's light is still to come. The students snuggled into the sheets and peacefully sleeping as the morning bells were yet to ring. James was asleep and suddenly a dream-like vision emerged as he traveled to bright light, and walked to his childhood home opening the main door. He walks upstairs and into the master bedroom seeing his mother lifeless on the bed just as he remembered the last time he saw his mother with the two maids and a priest. This time the priest was exactly Father Tolmen and the two maids turned to the pale-looking witches that changed the maid uniform to the ragged robes and hands that looked pale, boney, and pointed long nails. The morning bells rang to start the day, and James opened his eyes with the distraction of the bells from the nightmare breathing heavily as he was lying on the bed. He sat on the bed and rubbing his face from his hands stepping to the floor feeling the coldness as his feet were out of the covers until he slips into the white bedroom slippers.

The day is also the day that rises for the president and the vice president of the Phrontistery to be engaged one on one with the matter brought to them by James and his friends. Professor Galdor is insightful especially about procedures, laws, and systems in both the human world and the Pinnacle of Aries. He was talented to find the needful information to sort it right, and most importantly sort it for good. Professor Cuppins is always someone hardworking and committed to doing the best for the Phrontistery. She seems to be one steamy and high tempered, grumpy, or even hardly pleased by a lot of things, but never fails in the side of empathy towards anyone. Professor Cuppins travels to the town of Mr. Carter's address wearing some ordinary clothes worn in the human world in the formal attire of class and rich. A lady who is looking for a decent place to reside is her character played as she visits Mr. Carter's house in the hunt for information.

She knocks on the door and a man opens the door looking at Professor Cuppins. He wore a brown leather jacket, a dark green sweater with a pair of denim trousers.

"Good morning—are you Mr. Carter?"

"Good morning to you—may I know what is it regarding?"

"I am to look for a place to move in."

"Oh yes—I suppose you're looking for Mr. Allston Carter. I am his brother Arlo Carter—please come in."

"Thank you," said Professor Cuppins as she walking to an old simple English house.

"Are you into real estate as well?" asked Professor Cuppins.

"Oh no—I am into supplying for the movie business. I have a company that rents cameras, lightings, and sound equipment. My brother just went around the corner—he got some tenants to show one of the places down the street—he will arrive anytime now. Please have a seat miss."

"Thank you," said Mrs. Cuppins as she sits on the light-printed sofa.

Passing about fifteen minutes a man opened the door and walked in. It was Mr. Carter in a charcoal black suit finely dressed. His brother walked from inside the house out of the doorway.

"Ah, Allston—you have a guest."

Mr. Carter turned around and smiled at Professor Cuppins as he walks up to her reaching out his hand for a formal handshake.

"Hello good morning to you Miss—My name is Carter—Allston Carter. I believe you are here to see me"

"Yes—good morning I am Miss Cuppins " Said Professor Cuppins as she stands up to introduce herself.

"Nice to meet you Miss Cuppins—how may I help you?"

"I am looking for a place to buy and move in soon—someplace quiet and a bit away from the urban and the rush."

"Of course—there are few places, and one right past the town that's ideal to what you are looking for— spacious lawn and away from a dash of vehicles or hubbub from the town."

"That's lovely—I have a place in mind. I was told it was on sale about a month ago and it belonged to some reliable people."

"Where about?"

"It's called Wimbly Hills Residencies," said Professor Cuppins calmly. The name surprised Mr. Carter and turned to disappointment.

"It is a lovely place—and the first buyers saw eye to eye with the offer without any negotiations."

"Is it brought by a family?"

"Oh no—it was brought for some academic purpose as a research faculty if I am not mistaken. May I ask who told you about the place?"

"I am a good friend of the deceased owner—Mrs. Johanna Spinner. I was told by one of the mutual friends who also knows Johanna, and I was told the house was to be sold for education for Johanna's only son."

Mr. Carter's face turned to confusion after slightly been surprised with raised eyebrows.

"Are you sure you knew about selling this house a month ago?" asked Mr. Carter curiously.

"Yes—any problem Mr. Carter?' asked Professor Cuppins in a way that can be hardly suspected. Mr. Carter was looking down on the floor in deep thought and looks up in dismay.

"I do not know if you know this Miss Cuppins but the previous owner's son of the house—Miss Spinner's son who is the beneficiary died in an accident."

"But he is living with Mrs. Walsh—her sister."

"He used to—after the boy's passing, they adopted a child. To my knowledge, I think it was even before they had their daughter."

"How can you be so sure Mr. Carter? End of the day this boy owns the house, and there is a Trust Will to my knowledge—I was told by Johanna herself. I believe there should some document to prove his death."

Mr. Carter looked at Professor Cuppins suspiciously with his eyelids narrowing his eyes and head slightly tilted back.

"May I know why exactly you are here Miss Cuppins? Are you a relation to the Spinner family?"

"No I am not related—but a true friend is just like family."

Mr. Carter remains silent looking at Professor Cuppins with a sense of curiosity but also half convinced.

"What if I tell you that people can do many things—even lie about a person's existence?" asked Professor Cuppins with a strong eye contact that senses great confidence.

"I believe there could be a possibility—are you implying that this boy is alive?"

"Mr. Carter I do not doubt your expertise as a realtor, but I am sure you know there are many things between people, communities even family that could be personal—yet relevant. I would like to see proof that my late dear friend Miss Johanna Spinner's only son who has not yet come of age to even fight or voice against a legal matter if a lie was set up on his existence." Professor Cuppins demanded strongly.

Mr. Carter remained silent leaving a few seconds to pass as he also had a slight doubt of the boy's death from the point of hearing from the person on the Trust Will, and there is no reason to refuse to show the documents to Professor Cuppins.

"Miss Cuppins I believe you made a fair point to show evidence, as a person who knows the original owner of the house personally and her family so well. I suppose it is no harm done if these papers are legit to accept—after all, I am in this business for over thirty years and my reputation and trust are my reliability for being the best in this business." Said Mr. Carter calmly and with a sense of pride as he walks into the house bringing a letter-sized envelope taking out a paper and handed it over to Professor Cuppins. It was a copy of a death certificate and the name was stated at James Spinner. The date of the accident was stated as the seventeenth of September nineteen ninety four, and Professor Cuppins nodded her face side to side seeing the false evidence.

"I believe you received this from Mrs. Walsh is it?"

"Yes"

"May I have a copy of this certificate Mr. Carter?"

"It is a confidential document Miss Cuppins—but since you seem to know something more than what I was told by the family of the late beneficiary I suppose it will be alright. I have an extra copy in my office— please excuse me." Said Mr. Carter as he walked into his office room, and takes out the copy from a file on the office desk, and returns it to Professor Cuppins.

"Thank you Mr. Carter—I will call you if I come across anything which might be useful for you."

"Well thank you Miss Cuppins—I appreciate it!"

Professor Cuppins walked out of the door of the house of Mr. Carter with agitation looking at the certificate as she walks. "How dare you Tolmen!" she muttered as she walks fast behind a tall bush fence. She quickly takes out the power stone from her purse and wears the long silver chain with the glowing power stone on her chest. She takes a handful of glowing sand inside a little brown medicine bottle and throws the sand to her feet saying "Aries raferogus." As a skilled enchantress with a power stone that is powerful by mastering and wisdom to teach the future enchanters and enchantresses she lands exactly at the right place which is at the Phrontistery in front of Professor Galdor's office.

Chapter Thirteen: The Persuading Gospel

Professor Cuppins knocks on the door of Professor Galdor's office taking a deep breath and exhaling to calm herself for the pressure built with the furiousness towards Father Tolmen.

"Come in," said Professor Galdor in his usual calm and gravelly voice.

Professor Cuppins opened the door walking fast into the room.

"Sir I can't believe it—they having to be part of this almighty land of Aries are such traders—traders I tell you! Can you believe that Rebecca provided false evidence to prove James died in some fatal accident and there is no beneficiary to the house? Thank goodness the boy is with us and his future is written to be a part of the Pinnacle of Aries. I just cannot imagine what would happen otherwise to that poor child." Exclaimed Professor Cuppins as she burst with words out of pressure feeling disappointed for James, and the betrayal did to their dear student.

"Calm down Professor Cuppins—I understand that you genuinely feel downhearted for the student's matters especially when things lack Justice. I think we are willing to go an extra mile of care for James led by the special place in our heart for Johanna."

"I am sorry sir—I didn't mean to overreact."

"That's alright! Did you receive anything solid to convince the Bureau?"

"Yes sir," Said Professor Cuppins as she takes out a folded copy of the death certificate from her purse and handed it over to Professor Galdor.

"I got a copy of the proof documents provided to conceal the rights of the property to James. He is right sir—Father Tolmen is involved in this deal."

"Is it confirmed?"

"Certainly sir—Mr. Carter specifically said the place was brought for an academic purpose. I am sure he means the task we allocated to Father Tolmen."

"Good work Professor Cuppins! That's sure will be justifiable to let the undergraduate student for this matter due to the rights for the property."

"Sir—what exactly do you think the reason for Father Tolmen to buy the house belonging to James? It certainly not the only property set available to buy!" asked Professor Cuppins while Professor Galdor walked back and forth in front of his massive office desk slowly in some deep thought. Professor Cuppins's eyes follow him as he walks waiting for an answer in a perturbing look.

"I am sure there are many things we are not aware of as yet Professor Cuppins—but one thing is clear as the crystal waters of Adam's Ale!

Burton's greatest threat is James—a student to be a great and a powerful enchanter blessed by born powers of the Spirit Dragon."

"If the reason for purchasing the house that belongs to James is to get him as the target—then it is a great danger to involve James even if we get the approval from the Bureau." Said professor Cuppins in great concern as she slightly looked down and back at Professor Galdor.

"Unquestionably yes Professor Cuppins—a great danger indeed. But sooner or later the only person who could fight the witch tribe is the one blessed with the special powers. I wish we knew why Johanna gave up her power stone when she could have easily saved herself even though Burton must be fought years after. "That thought had crossed my mind countless times too sir."

In the study room, James was thinking and lost in his world as he looks outside the large window. Laura and the Davis brothers wrote some notes with their textbooks open, and Laura sucked into the book while she reads as usual. The room had many students but not too crowded, and all were either studying as they were supposed to in a study room, or reading while a few softly does the chitter-chatter. Laura sights James as he seems to be thinking looking out through the window. She walked up to James and stood behind him as she looks at him concernedly.

"James! You were standing here for some time now—are you alright?"

"Yes, I was just wondering what Professor Galdor did regarding Father Tolmen and my mother's house used by the evil."

Before Laura could respond a student walked towards them from outside the study room and said that Professor Cuppins wants James to visit her at the corner classroom of the Adam's Ale practice room.

James walked into the practice room, and the room had benches made as a stadium around the room like a sports stadium with a wide opening of the roof in the middle. It had a flow of water that flows at the center opening of the roof, and it flows to the floor as the water disappears to the ground. As usual, the powers of Adam's Ale could create a waterfall, river, lake, or stream that constantly flows even indoors without a drop spilled around the strong water flow. There was a line of radiant color that moves like a ribbon inside the water, and the water sparkles as the light reflect on the water as crystal drops. Professor Cuppins was seated at the lowest bench a bit far from the entrance as she speaks to one of the reception elves who was standing

in front of her. They were both eye to eye as the elf lady was standing and Professor Cuppins seated at the

long curved benches. James entered the room as Professor Cuppins concluded her conversation. The elf lady

nodded and left the classroom wobbling back out of the door.

"James!"

"Good morning Professor Cuppins—I was told you wished to see me."

"Yes, come in."

"James I wanted to speak to you about an important matter."

 "What is it, Professor?"

"I went to speak to the realtor—Mr. Carter yesterday—the one who did the deal to your mother's house to

Father Tolmen through your aunt. I am truly sorry for everything you had to witness and come across, and I

understand how difficult it might be for you. I've got proof that we believe will be adequate for the Bureau

to allow us to give you authority to involve you—and in handling the matter by going to the house. But I

should warn you James—this is a very dangerous thing."

"I understand Professor—fighting or to do deal with that has anything to do with Burton is risky."

"Yes but not just that James!" Said Professor Cuppins calmly while looking at James concernedly at the

same time. James was confused about what is more dangerous apart from dealing with Burton and his fight

for justice. Little did he know how source powers work in the human world, and it is never a wise way to

fight or deal with the evil stepping out from the Pinnacle of Aries.

"James—I want you to understand this carefully, and it will be useful for you in the future. The human world

is very far from the land of Aries even though we travel to it fast as an escape velocity with the powers of the

glowing sand. The source powers of a power stone are not at the highest to fight such a strong power such as

the witchcrafts and burton's—strengthened by your mother's power stone. It is impossible to fight evil

without the powers of the Spirit Dragon."

"But Professor Cuppins—I don't understand why is it that I have to fight without the powers of the Spirit

Dragon?"

"The Spirit Dragon can advise you, but the frequency for the worlds is different—the Spirit Dragon cannot come through you to fight Burton or witchcraft in the human world. You will learn on the frequencies and things in depth once you qualify to the post-graduate faculty years."

"What can we do Professor?"

"If we have to fight this we have to bring Father Tolmen here—the Pinnacle of Aries."

The afternoon was relaxed and free as in the schedule, but the opposite of James as he was seated at the meeting room with Professor Galdor, Professor Cuppins, Professor Sisko, and Professor Lansford with two men from the Bureau. Both were middle-aged men wearing black clerical sack suits that seem to be having a great relationship that's amiable yet formal with the faculty management, especially with Professor Galdor. However, it is a difficult task to easily convince just by the basis of trust to accept an undergraduate student's involvement.

"Professor Galdor—you and the management of the Phrontistery has a great reputation for years with the Bureau. Never for all these years have you brought such an appalling request to approve for your authority. Do you understand the risk involved in this matter—whoever the family is or whatever the power the undergraduate student consists?" said one of the men looking displeased at Professor Galdor.

"We understand—but we are to be faced in a much dangerous situation. The power stones in the human world can be easily searched with the powers of Miss Johanna Spinner's power stone and witchcraft powers. The power stones of many enchanters and enchantresses is a combination of an undefeatable power, also a mix of many skills and abilities of the owners once their consciousness is taken to the power stones."

"What if the owner is deceased with old age—how much danger are we talking about?" asked one of the officials in the Bureau.

"We believe there is a much greater risk to the future enchanters and enchantresses who are yet to step to the Pinnacle of Aries." Said Professor Cuppins.

"How is that Professor Cuppins?" asked the man as he frowns with curiosity.

"Taking the consciousness of the future enchanters and enchantresses in the human world to avoid their powers to be mastered here. It will be difficult to cure in any way, if these children are in the human world we will not know to find them." Replied Professor Cuppins.

"If you could recall officials— few of our undergraduate students had the unfortunate experience during the attack of the Phrontistery. One of the student's consciousness was taken not to return to the body. We cannot imagine what would have happened if it's not for this undergraduate student"

"How did you bring the consciousness back?" asked the official from James. The men representing the Bureau tried their best to find even the simplest fact to justify that James's involvement is not necessary, and do not give much concern to what's happening in the human world by Burton.

"We understand that the Bureau focuses within the boundaries of the Pinnacle of Aries, and the only focus concerning us is the Phrontistery. We've got records that most of the enchanters or enchantresses who left the Pinnacle of Aries to live back in the human world did not die of old age—their consciousness was taken making them weak and lifeless both physically and emotionally." Said Professor Sisko.

"If we send this young boy who is still studying in the first year as an undergraduate can help such a serious matter—that is in the human world? Asked the other official who remained silent most of the time during the discussion in a sarcastic manner looking at James with a stare that made James slightly uncomfortable.

"Yes that is right," said Professor Galdor confidently.

"Fine—but why is it important to go to the human world or the house? If this property was brought for the Phrontistery—we assume you must be having an agreement with Father Tolmen to transfer the property once the purchasing of the place is complete?" asked one of the officials looking at Professor Galdor and turning to Professor Cuppins.

"Yes we do," replied Professor Cuppins calmly.

"Great! So why not sell the place to just some ordinary family or some person in the human world—or even destroy it if there is a risk tied in living there with the presence of the witches in the house?" said one of the officials.

"No!" exclaimed James breathing heavily and looking worried. The officials looked at James surprised by the unexpected response.

Professor Galdor and Professor Cuppins looked at each other with mettle as they fixed their mind to come to the point of the house. The Bureau's focus and concerns stay within the place of their work, and it was well aware by the management of the Phrontistery.

"This was the other important point to address in this meeting with the Bureau—regard the house." Said Professor Galdor.

"What would that be Professor Galdor?" Said one of the officials that speaks the most leaning forward to listen closely.

"The ownership of the house—it belonged to Miss Johanna Spinner and her son is the beneficiary."

The officials looked at James confusedly and to Professor Galdor glancing back at James.

"How did this happen? You are not even at the legally accepted age to take any decision of selling the house in the first place!" Asked the official-looking at James gathering his eyebrows together.

James looked at Professor Galdor and back at the two gentlemen representing the Bureau.

"It was not my decision." Replied James nervously in a soft voice.

Professor Galdor took out a paper from a file on the table underneath his hands.

"There is a testamentary will to the house under Rebecca Spinner—the only sister of Johanna Spinner who never came back to the Pinnacle of Aries from the human world after she fully graduated from the Phrontistery. There was no track of her identity since she made sure her power stone was not renewed or in power to avoid Burton from tracing her. I can assure you that even she is under great danger since no power stone can be fully unpowered, and the only way we found her or the fact that she is in danger is through James.

"How did she sell the property?" asked one of the officials curiously.

"She made false evidence that the beneficiary is no longer alive. We have proof which she had provided to the realtor." Said Professor Galdor as he pushes the paper on the surface of the polished table to the official seated next to him. He picked up the paper looking at it carefully fixing his round pair of glasses. He seems to be slightly in shock as he gives the paper to the other official-looking at James with one eyebrow raised, and staring without uttering a word. The other official runs through the details on the paper and looks up at James and Professor Galdor.

"Could it be that your aunt is helping Burton?" asked the official.

"No! Please you don't understand she trusted Father Tolmen." Said James furiously.

"We understand she is your family, but right now we have a greater concern in taking the right decisions to sort this mess. How can you assure your aunt is not in the side of Burton, son?" asked one of the officials. James was looking at him with eyes wide as he didn't know how to convince the two men representing the Bureau.

"Didn't we all trust Father Tolmen that he would be suitable to join the management and the lecture board of the Phrontistery?" asked Professor Lansford calmly. The only words uttered by Professor Lansford after a long silence throughout the meeting, but also a point rich as gold to convince the men that the events could also be the possibility of Rebecca Spinner now under the family name of Walsh has nothing to do with Burton.

"Fine we understand that there is the level of distress regarding the house for the student personally—however I am still unclear on what business does the management have on behalf of the Phrontistery to involve an undergraduate?" asked the other official from Professor Galdor with a glance at James.

"Let me handle matter about Father Tolmen in the human world—I promise you it will save the Pinnacle of Aries, and the house should be removed from his doings as well as the witches." Said James with a voice that showed his courage and determination.

"I am afraid we cannot go against the regulations of the Bureau. This is an issue regarding a key person in the management." said the official nodding with disappointment.

"We may keep this discussion within these walls where the top management of the Bureau has no say in the human world." Said Professor Galdor with a stabbing stare as the official nodded agreeing with a sly.

"You have to keep your word son—in the human world—only! Understand?" said the official-looking at James raising his bushy eyebrow.

"Yes—I promise."

The meeting was finally over with a hard round to convince the bureau to allow James to fight in a way different to how an academic organization that overlooks almost everything and as the final authoritative body would handle. It was a great relief to James as well as the faculty management to convey the importance of the house, and the reason for going back to the human world to undo the plans of the evil that is undoubtedly necessary.

It was a class unsettled, noisy, and yet to begin as the students were Laura was reading her textbooks while the Davis brothers were chatting with some boys in the class as they were all free-standing, sitting on chairs and one on the table. James took his seat next to Laura taking a deep breath closing his eyes. Even though his response was courageous and firm in the meeting it was at the classroom that he finally catches some breath relaxing with the strong tension that played in him having to convince the officials of the bureau.

"James! What happened?" asked Laura and the Davis brothers walked up to him fully curious to know what happened in the meeting.

"It was a close one—the Bureau gave permission for my involvement in Father Tolmen's matter, and accepted to go back to the house under the faculty's knowledge and permission."

"Oh James that is great news!" Said Laura excitedly.

"Phew—that's great news indeed." Said Mathew while taking his seat as the rest of the students rushed to their places with Professor Cuppins walking into the classroom.

"Good afternoon students—first off there is an announcement to make. We will have the annual Sports day competition in March, and we have been having his special event for over fifty years of the Phrontistery. It is held between congresses, and your skills and performance will be scored to your reports. Each congress will be scored in total, and awarded by the Bureau of Academics and Sports. The winning congress and the performers are surely the top stories of the Pinnacle of Aries among anyone in the city, place, or homes."

A student raised her hand at the back row of the class eager to ask a question after hearing Professor Cuppins's announcement and brief.

"Yes, Miss Harley?"

"Professor Cuppins—which congress won the very first time that held this event?"

"Well—the very first year was won by us the Phrontistery."

"Pardon me for interrupting Professor Cuppins, but which congress won the very first year of this event Professor?" asked one of the students.

"Back then how this event and day held was different—the participants were different, the game structure was different, and mostly who competed with whom was different. In the first years of this the Phrontistery, even the Pinnacle of Aries was different. We and the Witchcrafts were in harmony, and there was nothing to fear of them stepping into our world or us to the wizarding world.

Years back before one of the very first enchanters used witchcraft's hidden dark magic for the greed to power was where everything changed. The Phrontistery competed with the Wizard school with fair, skillful, and an entertaining event to everyone." After Professor Cuppins explained she was distracted in deep thought in a very few seconds of silence. She soon came back to the class and looked around the student walking to the front of the class.

"Alright—now this is about the sports event that we will be expecting your participation without obligation but in your own will. The participant's skills will be evaluated to your overall annual performance records in your report books. Now the game is structured into three parts that will be played using the source powers of your congress. I will introduce the coach tomorrow as he is unable to attend today—for now, I will give you a summary of the game. You will all be separated into three groups depending on your source powers gravel, Adams Ale, and Welkin. The race will be starting with a player from each congress, and at the finishing line of the round the other team player of your congress will complete the next round—likewise, there will be three rounds to complete. There will be twenty-one players selected for this event from one congress, and ten individuals that will be competing with each other in the same congress in each round. The best performance of the three rounds will award the winning congress, and the ten individuals will be scored for the participants scoring to overall performance in the annual student reports."

The students were listening with great interest yet confused with how the game is scored or structured. It was no surprise for Professor Cuppins that it is a confusion to a new badge that has no idea of the game held annually by Phrontistery. After class James had no interest in the game but to rush to Professor Galdor's office.

"Sir, when can I go to the house?"

"Whenever you are ready James because it's a place that belongs to you personally—but I decided that you will not be going alone this time, and I decided to send Phanto with you."

"Thank you, sir, I was hoping to go the earliest. Today itself—sir."

"Of course. Come back sharp at eleven, and I will ask Phanto to be prepared—Oh and James!"

"Yes sir."

"Do wear something that will look ordinary to the human world."

"Yes sir."

James left the door with great agitation knowing that it will be a great challenge going back to the house to fight with Father Tolmen. After the clock ticks sharp eleven in the fine morning, and the gold liquid fills the water clock on the Phrontistery roof fills to the carved eleven. Phanto walked up to James as he was about to open Professor Galdor's office.

Phanto and James walked into Professor Galdor's office seeing him and Professor Cuppins waiting for them. Professor Galdor is standing in front of his seat, and Professor Cuppins is next to the visitor chairs facing the door looking at Phanto and James walking into the office.

"As I said James you will not be going alone—Phanto will come along, and as well as Professor Cuppins."

"Sir—I appreciate it but Father Tolmen will never accept his true identity in front of the management of the Phrontistery."

"Oh don't you worry about that! Come along now we shouldn't take too much time to chit chat." Said Professor Cuppins as she walked past them out of the office.

They appeared in the human world with Phanto wearing an ordinary suit with Professor Cuppins in some clothes of a working woman, and James in a pair of trousers, sneakers, a t-shirt, and a blue jacket. The name Wimberley Hills Residence was all they needed to be said with a splash of glowing sand to be standing in the human world and front of James's childhood home. They didn't need to walk forward and be thrown back with a skilled master, and a spirit pixie with great knowledge and senses.

"The land is protected from entering!" said Phanto.

"Yes! But how do you know?" asked James stunned.

"I can sense it—and I can also sense it is not some source power." Said Phanto with a glance at Professor Cuppins.

"There is one way to enter." Said James leading them to the middle of a sidewall with a crack that was found following the row of ants walking into the land from the woods.

"How did you get in James?" asked Professor Cuppins calmly observing the wall.

"We jumped over the wall Professor Cuppins."

"Well that would be fun if it was my glorious younger days—I will get an awful crack in my back!" said Professor Cuppins sarcastically as she took out her power stone inside the purse. The glowing yellow power stone was beaming with light as the strength of its powers are active and mastered for years. Professor Cuppins aimed the power stone at the wall as a beam of yellow light raised a few bricks at the bottom of the wall effortlessly like raising a fabric. James was looking at the curved wall with space at the bottom enough to crawl to the other side moved by the strong powers of Professor Cuppins's power stone. The challenge is to begin by fighting the evil beyond the tall strong gates and the walls protecting the house and the lawn without a trim or a slight nurturing for years.

Chapter Fourteen: A Prideful Defeat

James was staring at the wall curved upwards from the ground to crawl to the other side, the pat was felt slightly pushing him forwards towards the wall by Professor Cuppins.

"Go on now!" said Professor Cuppins.

James crawled to the other side of the wall and Phanto after Professor Cuppins crawled to the lawn of the house.

Professor Cuppins aimed the power stone towards the wall as the curve was lowered and the base of the wall was on the ground as it should be.

"There is a window on the side—we can get in through the maid's room if it's not locked." Said James as he was stopped by Professor Cuppins while he was about to leave to check the window.

"We will enter nowhere else but from the main entrance!" said Professor Cuppins as she walked passing Phanto and James towards the main door of the house. James and Phanto looked at each other slightly confused following her to the main entrance of the house.

Professor Cuppins rang the bell on the side of the door frame finely molded with iron with a bell at the edge of the curved iron pole that had a row of five pigeons which was crafted as the birds were standing on the top of the pole. Father Tolmen opened the door, and as soon as he sees Professor Cuppins he had a wide smile and turned to look at Phanto with a smile slightly less than what he had. Phanto and Professor Cuppins remained expressionless looking at Father Tolmen, and it seemed obvious that Father Tolmen purposely disregarded James's presence with them.

"Professor Cuppins! The day is full of lovely surprises—there are few arrangements left. I was planning to come back to the faculty tomorrow or the day after." Said Father Tolmen as he stepped aside from the doorway allowing Professor Cuppins, Phanto, and James to walk in.

"Welcome Phanto—it's very rare to see you in the human world!" said Father Tolmen while Phanto and Professor Cuppins remained calm.

"How do you do Father Tolmen—what are the pending arrangements?" Professor Cuppins asked while she turns her head observing the interior of the house.

"Oh, just some renovations Professor Cuppins!" Father Tolmen replied calmly. James was trembling with anger, and his hands were shivering with rage while he frowns at Father Tolmen about to burst with furiousness. Phanto felt that James was no longer on a level to cope if he was not stopped before he reacts with his emotions building up. Phanto walked towards James and held his shoulder to encourage him to calm himself while Professor Cuppins and Father Tolmen were in a conversation.

"This house seems just beautiful—how did you get to know about this place?" Professor Cuppins asked calmly.

"I have a friend who is in the real estate business who knows a realtor—that was the contact I provided to Professor Galdor before I left to get a place."

"Who are the previous owners?"

"A family I suppose. It belonged to a beneficiary, and a trust will is given to one of the original owner's family members."

"Did the beneficiary sell the house?" asked Phanto.

"No he died!" said Father Tolmen looking at Phanto and Professor Cuppins.

"That is very unfortunate indeed! But what if we tell you that it isn't true Father Tolmen." Said Professor Cuppins as she observed Father Tolmen's reactions closely.

"Pardon!" uttered Father Tolmen narrowing his eyes.

Professor Cuppins took out the copy of the death certificate and showed it to Father Tolmen holding the paper right in front of his eyes.

"I am sure you knew everything before we have to explain a word to you Father Tolmen—so tell me since when did you decide to switch sides of power being a spirit guide?"

"Which side do you imply that I stand on Professor Cuppins?" asked Father Tolmen silently with a cunning lopsided grin.

"The side that uses the black ash dust of witchcrafts surrounding the walls of this property of course." Said Professor Cuppins with a frown and a stare that strikes through his eyes. However, it was obvious that Father Tolmen is hardly bothered about anything uttered to him even exposing his true identity.

"You are a liar and a traitor! It was you next to my mother's bed the day I was taken away by my aunt wasn't it?" exclaimed James. Phanto and Professor Cuppins turned to James with great shock.

James walked up to Father Tolmen slowly as he looked straight into his disingenuous eyes.

"Give me the power stone!" said James.

"What if I prefer not to?"

"Then you will face many consequences!" said Professor Cuppins.

"Are you threatening me, child?"

"No! We are commanding you—in the name of justice with the powers of Aries we command you to give in," shouted Phanto using his powers aiming his palms to the wooden floor.

A few wood planks tore from the floor as the wood all combined forming a strong and crafted lion that walked towards Father Tolmen roaring looking at him as if it's the perfect prey. The lion jumped onto Father Tolmen as it grabbed his hand with its sharp teeth pushing Father Tolmen to the ground. Father Tolmen kept fighting the lion pushing it and trying his best to get out of its capture. After a few seconds, the lion disappeared into dust letting Father Tolmen stand up on his feet.

"The power is insufficient to fight in the human world." Said Professor Cuppins while she, Phanto, and James was standing with a great alert looking at Father Tolmen.

Father Tolmen took out the power stone in the pocket of his robe and aimed it towards them as they were pushed with great power and force towards the wall. They were thrown to the wall and fell helplessly hard on the floor.

Phanto quickly got on his feet helping Professor Cuppins to stand while looking at James who was slowly and painfully standing on his own with a cut making the side of his forehead bleed.

"James are you alright?" asked Phanto concernedly holding Professor Cuppins.

James did not respond but was looking around disturbed while Phanto and Professor Cuppins looked around following James. Five witches were surrounding them staring at them as the wind blows strongly with the energy of witchcraft making their long white hair flowing behind them. They looked pale and cold-blooded in their skin, and they put their hands out with their palms aiming at Professor Cuppins, Phanto, and James. A black smoke traveled towards them in a great force as the smoke was moving fast. Phanto used his powers with his hands aiming with his palms using a glowing yellow light that stopped the smoke from getting closer to them while Professor Cuppins aimed at the smoke with the glowing yellow light that comes out of her power stone in her hands. James grabbed the gold-plated iron Thonet coat stand on the side stabbing the witch in front of him with the pointed design on the top of the stand as a spear. She disappeared with an echoing scream into the thin air which took the attention of the witch standing next to the one who disappeared. She aimed the witchcraft smoke towards James as the smoke was now away from the protected light cover and traveled fast aiming at James. James quickly jumped to the side and ran towards the stairs and up the stairs as fast as he could. The witch turned around and aimed the black smoke towards James as traveled behind James aiming at him fast as a lightning strike. Phanto used the coat stand on the floor and threw it at the witch facing the other side aiming at James. The coat stand stabbed the witch as she fell on the floor with the smoke vanishing as her power was stopped. She fell on the floor and disappeared with an echoing scream and vanished. There were now only three witches left that were attacking Phanto and Professor Cuppins.

Meanwhile, James ran upstairs and ran into the master bedroom locking himself in the room.

"Master! Please I need your help."

He heard the echoing soothing voice of the spirit dragon through the walls.

"I am here James!" said the voice of the spirit dragon.

"Master I need your help—tell me how I can stop him!"

"Who do you mean he?" asked the spirit dragon.

"Father Tolmen—if I stop him he cannot bring the dead witches to attack us."

"There is no power over a man that is molded without a soul James."

"I do not understand master! What is it that has the power to stop Father Tolmen?"

"All you need to do is to break the chain of the death beads and place the death bead at the prayer symbol. Whatever you will see or hear will be a challenge, and if you do as I've guided you—you will succeed." Said the voice of the Spirit Dragon while it vanished as the voice slightly decreased in the last three words. James felt that the spirit dragon is done telling him what he needs to do, and it is now his turn to somehow stop Father Tolmen at all cost.

The lock on the door fell as the heavy iron lock made a loud sound hitting the wooden planks on the floor distracting James. The door opened with ease with Father Tolmen standing behind the door frame outside the room looking at James with his usual calmness. James surprisingly noticed that his hand the spirit animal attacked is without a drop of blood. The sleeve of the robe was torn but without a scratch on his arm.

"Father Tolmen you've done enough—just stop this!" said James with Father Tolmen walking slowly through the room closer to James.

"I am sure you've got some fond memories of this place." Said Father Tolmen taking a look around and back to James.

"It was you, wasn't it? The day I was taken away… You were behind all of this."

"There are many things you haven't yet understood dear child. Burton is not a…"

"Burton!" exclaimed James.

"What are you talking about? He killed my mother—and you are helping him."

"James you just need to open your eyes a little bit and see the wonders of witchcraft."

"Stop! Give me the power stone."

"What are you talking about?"

"You know exactly what I am talking about."

"James I do not have your mother's power stone."

"I know that! I am asking for your power stone attached to a chain of death beads." Said James and Father Tolmen slightly turned his head to look at James with a smile.

"I am impressed! You are aware of many things!" said Father Tolmen, and it was clear that by now James is about to pass his level of patience. He used his powers and grew in strong branches of the trees that surrounds the house breaking through the windows around the room, and it all wrapped around Father Tolmen. The branches held his arms and body making him still while James walked towards him.

"Listen James—I know you are very wise but this will not help you!"

"Give me the power stone with the chain of death beads." Shouted James.

Father Tolmen used his powers with eyes focused on James and burst the branches destroying them as it turned into dust falling to the floor.

Right after two witches emerged from the floor on the two sides of Father Tolmen, and they walked towards James taking a step after another slowly with their eyes beaming of evil. The powers of James with the presence of the Spirit Dragon's blessings cannot fight as he was in the human world. A powerful enchanter as James is still to discover and master his skills of Gravel being born blessed with powers of the Spirit Dragon. It was a moment of great danger and proving the powers of light and darkness. Three dangerous witchcrafts against one boy who is not yet holding his power stone but learning to be an enchanter, and limited powers from his master to fight had nothing else to do than taking steps backward when Father Tolmen and the three witches walked towards him.

The room was bright and suddenly an unexplained gloominess covered the room disappearing the light from the all the windows. He hears a strong thunder that strikes around the house, and beams of lights from the thunder strike that was gradient in bright red and gold hit James's body as it glows bright from head to toe. It was unexplainable and confusing to anyone including the witchcraft. The light of his body was now away and he looked his usual self except was more fearless, strong, and powerful in the gloominess of the room. He aimed his palms in front of them with eyes intrepid looking strongly at Father Tolmen. The strong lightning of color-like fire was thrown from the center of James's palms attacking the witches. The cold eyes of the witches were wide seeming to be fearful and helpless when the lightning strikes was about to attack them. Father Tolmen seemed shocked looking at the two witches that turned into ashes as their screams disappeared. The ashes on the floor were dusted for the strong wind as the windows open so fast as it was about to tear off from its window frames, and the silk curtains moves flowing its fabric. James stood no longer fearless and the strength of his powers was visible in his eyes that stared at Father Tolmen without a blink.

Father Tolmen took out the power stone from the pocket of his robe with the chain of death beads hanging attached to the power stone. He held the power stone from both hands looking at the power stone and looked up at James. He quickly aimed the power stone at James and a flash of blue lightning surrounded with a black light and smoke came out the power stone trying to attack James. Father Tolmen staring at James with great rage and his evil eyes focusing on James to fight him. James remained still until the powers of the witchcraft and power stone were halfway towards James. He blocked the lightning strike in the black light beam and smoke with his bare palms holding it stopping it to go through him with all his might.

Phanto and Professor Cuppins ran to the master bedroom escaping from the witches looking at James in shock. After holding on to the evil powers for a couple of seconds the beam of light turned yellow with the black smoke disappearing, and the lightning strike turned red towards Father Tolmen. The power stone strengthened with witchcraft spells was protecting Father Tolmen as he was holding the power stone before his chest with all his strength. The powers of Pinnacle of Aries and born blessed by the spirit dragon were too powerful as it covered the power stone losing its evil witchcraft powers and through Father Tolmen. The powers made Father Tolmen scream in fear and pain as he turned to molded clay statue and melted to the floor. The chain attached to the power stone burst with the death beads falling to the wooden floor. "Of course—no power over a man molded without a soul," James uttered to himself in a soft voice looking at the clay melting on the surface of the floor.

The witches' melted turning to a form of wet clay then turned to black ashes and finally to dust which was blown sweeping off the floor for the strong wind that blew right after the attack. The powers of James reduced restoring to himself as the gloominess of the room was lightened as the strong wind disappeared. James closed his eyes with the powers drifting away from him, and as he opened his eyes Phanto and Professor Cuppins were staring at James in great shock with the tiniest movement. James now seems calmer and peaceful as he looked at Professor Cuppins and Phanto at the door to the master bedroom.

"James!" said Professor Cuppins remaining shocked as they both walked into the room and stood in front of James.

"James are you hurt?" asked Phanto

"I'm fine."

"This is a miracle!" muttered professor Cuppins. James noticed Phanto and Professor Cuppins were staring at him surprised.

"What is it?" asked James doubtfully.

"James—you are born blessed powerful than what we could imagine!" said Phanto

Professor Cuppins looking closely at James stepped forward with a surprising look.

As I mentioned to you at the Phrontistery—the spirit dragon can only guide you in the human world, but you seem to have powers that run through your veins which are powerful in all probability more than your mother or any other enchanter or enchantress to this day." Said Professor Cuppins.

"The death beads!" grunted James looking around the wooden floor. Phanto kneeled on the floor collecting every death bead fallen. James sighted the power stone and reached to pick up the power stone of Father Tolmen that was underneath the stool of the dressing table.

"No! Don't touch that!" said Phanto as he quickly stood and walked up to where James was kneeling and handed him the death beads. James stood up and walked fast towards the door.

"Where are you going James?" asked Professor Cuppins

"I have to keep it on the prayer symbol Professor Cuppins!" said James as he left the master bedroom and ran downstairs.

On his way to the room that had the prayer symbol of witchcraft, witches emerged from the stairs, hall, and corridor as he ran to the room downstairs. The witches were chasing him but James managed to run fast as he could with about six witches chasing him. He quickly opened the door to enter the room seeing the witches getting closer to him. He entered the room and so did the witches. He felt trapped and there was no way to escape as the witches have entered and blocked the door surrounding him. He takes steps backward when the witches take the steps towards him. James stepped on the prayer symbol drawn on the floor, and as soon as the witches sees his foot stepping on the drawn fine lines of the symbol, the witches stood where they were without a foot forward while looking worried. It was obvious at this point that they looked at the symbol and James fully with fear sensing the rightful power defeating the witchcraft. It was clear that the witches could not step or come near the symbol. James slowly takes the steps backward to the center of the symbol, and he crouched down about to put a few death beads at the center.

James was suddenly in a dark place with nothing visible, not even a door or furniture. It was fully dark as the starless night sky all around, and he sees his aunt tied to a chair right in front of him not more than three or four steps away. She looked exhausted with eyes drained as if she walked for miles in a hot dessert, and not an ounce of energy left. She was tied in a chain of death beads around her body and looked desperately at James.

"James help me!"

James looked at her shocked and there was nothing he could see apart from his aunt tied to a chair.

"James give those death beads to the witches, and they will free me. Please forgive me, James." Said Mrs. Walsh with tears oozing in her eyes of tiredness and exhausted.

James looked at the death beads in his hands and turned around to look at the witchcraft. The witches were awaiting staring with their pale skin and greyish eyes awaiting to have the death beads to their hands. James took a last look at his aunt as she was staring at him in pain and helplessness.

"James can you remember this?" said Mrs. Walsh showing a music box that was on her lap which was not there before. James recalled it as one of the things that brought his childhood memories of his mother. His mother used the sweet music to help him fall asleep. She used to turn the little handle on the side as it gives soothing music of a lullaby. When James was taken by his aunt he used to hear it often which was the music of happy memories when he was very little. But now it is one of the most painful memories, and James put it away years ago after he learned his mother passed away.

The music box was playing the familiar lullaby which made it a painful moment having to listen to it.

"Stop it—please!" shouted James at his aunt.

"Give them the death beads—I promise you the witches will leave, and I will never betray or lie to you ever again."

James recalled the words of the spirit dragon and he repeated to himself in the middle of being confused of what he sees and hear around him at the moment.

"Everything that you see or hear will be a challenge!" said James softly muttering the words of the Spirt Dragon to himself looking at the witches and his aunt in front of him.

James suddenly got into his senses as he looked at the prayer symbol and placed the death beads that were nowhere else but under the feet of his aunt made nothing more than an illusion to trap his mind to regain the powers of the evil.

A bright light beamed out of each line of the prayer symbol as the witches screamed in fear and everything around was visible around the house. The witches have disappeared, the painful illusion of his aunt tied to a chair is no longer visible. Phanto and Professor Cuppins came running into the room with great worry, and as soon as they sighted James with no harm the worrying faces changed to relief.

Professor Cuppins the power stone of Father Tolmen!" said James as he was about to leave the room in a hurry.

"Slow down child! The power stone is now secured under the powers and the blessings of the pinnacle of Aries." Said Professor Cuppins and Phanto showed the power stone which is no longer bright but just a stone or crystal.

"This needs to be kept in a safe place if not anything could be possible!" said Professor Cuppins looking concernedly at the power stone Phanto was holding in his hand.

"Can Burton or the Witchcrafts come back to attack us?" asked James full of curiosity making a line between his thick brows.

"A person named Father Tolmen may not be existing but could be remade by powers of evil-— witchcraft is a tribe that existed with powers of evil for decades. That is why the mistake of wrong spirt guide should not repeat. How they entered to harm the Phrontistery however was through the power stone of the Spirit Guide. After Father Luka's passing we provided the power stone to Father Tolmen. The Spirit Guide's power stone mastered for years that provides great access to the evil if it's in the wrong hands. Though no souls are at present of the witchcrafts, the dark powers exist anywhere. Besides let's not forget your mother's power stone is still with Burton" Said Professor Cuppins looking at James's worrisome face.

"Now let's not worry about that James! Let's get back to the Phrontistery as soon as we can.

The three appeared at the entrance of the Phrontistery and the midget man was facing one of the women elves buried in some conversation minding his own business. He quickly turned around and looked at them with great surprise mostly excited as he quickly wobbled towards them. He grabbed James from his arms and hugged him tightly as if he saw a dear friend or family who had arrived after years apart. As he let go he spoke with great excitement and a wide smile in a way James had never witnessed this old midget man so happy before.

"Oh, lad! You are a miracle I tell you—a miracle. You have brought the true meaning of the Pinnacle of Aries. That Tolmen—the ungrateful black hat and law break does not deserve in this land of the good."

 "Ehem" Professor Cuppins cleared her throat interrupting Mose as he expressed his rage on the injustice and the shower of compliments of James's doings.

"Sorry Professor Cuppins!"

Professor Cuppins, James, and Phanto walked towards the hallway and as they passed the counters the moving statues saluted them in respect mainly turning the finely crafted faces at James, and the elves stands bowing their heads looking at James with great appreciation.

Supper was arranged and the Phrontistery expects punctuality at its best especially from the students to not disturb the rest of the day's schedule. James was exhausted despite the freshened up long shower and fresh clothes after he arrived from all the events that he encountered in the human world.

He walks into the dining room and all students stare at him with great surprise while some girls whisper as he passes them. The Davis brothers and Laura looking excited and smiling was waiting for him to join leaving a seat empty next to Laura. James sits down while he looks at Laura and Davis brothers with his warm friendly smile.

"It's good to have you back James!" said Mathew.

In the background, James hears the familiar voice, and it's non-other than Professor Galdor.

"Attention students—as you may have all heard we have an amazing achievement to the Pinnacle of Aries by defeating the witchcraft and the evil powers that had been used within the Phrontistery itself causing great danger to the safety of all of us. This defeat is not just an achievement to the land of Aries but a recognition that brings pride and dignity to our faculty, and we are proud to see such talents and blessed future enchanters."

Professor Cuppins turned her head towards James smiling calmly at him, and the voice of Professor Galdor continued the announcement after great applause for the announcing of the defeat.

"The fine enchanter that we should especially thank for bringing safety back to the faculty is Mr. James Spinner in the Gravel congress."

The students cheered while applauding for James while it gave a great sense of happiness and self-pride to the boy that he never felt before.

Post supper the students were chatting walking out of the dining room while some were in the sides of the hallway chatting   with their friends within the short time permitted until the bells rings to get back to the congresses.

While James, Laura, and Davis brothers were slowly walking in the hallway Professor Sisko called out "James there you are!"

All four turned around to look at the call while Professor Sisko walked up to them with a wide smile on his face.

"How are you doing James?"

"I am fine Professor Sisko."

"I have to say James what you did was just astonishing and we are looking forward to seeing all of you be great in the land Aries."

"James—hope you are doing alright!" said Professor Galdor as he walked up and stood next to Professor Sisko.

"Yes sir, I am fine."

"James—since the matter regarding your mother's house is cleared it is now solely yours and your responsibility even though you are still to be that age to do anything about it." Said Professor Galdor calmly.

"Sir—I was thinking maybe you continue to use it for the place to find the power stones that you've assigned before. But there is a problem sir!" said James as he looked slightly disappointed.

"First of all it is very kind of you to offer your childhood home—what is it that bothers you?" asked Professor Galdor concernedly looking calmly at James.

"Sir the house is not in a state of use—windows shattered and broken, floors cracked and some planks are burned with the attack."

"Don't worry about it boy! We will repair everything good as new. Now go get yourselves some rest. Considering the event and what was encountered we have decided to give a two weeks break for students to go home and start new. We would start the faculty with the sports event to give some entertainment and activeness to the students for the start. We can have a revisit to your house James, and do the repairs within the two weeks."

"Sir—it all sounds just wonderful, but where would I go? My aunt—she will not welcome me worse than her husband for taking her power stone." Said James as he utters words with great sadness.

"Why would you need to be anywhere James? Your home is here—and we would always be pleased to have you with us despite if the faculty is on vacation or not." Said Professor Galdor while Professor Sisko slightly nods with the agreement with a light pleasing smile.

James was lying in his bed and felt a sense of great inner peace and happiness. It was a feeling of being where he belonged which he never felt in his years even though he lived with his relatives. He closes his eyes to sleep while his mind was thankful for everything feeling complete, and it is even more satisfying to finding his true self and purpose. Along with the self-satisfaction of doing the right actions, and most importantly saving his mother's house which was gifted to James as his own home was not more than experiencing being where he belonged. He feels the Phrontistery is his home so strong that he never felt before. He runs his mind about his purpose which is yet to be served, and it's more than clear to James that this is only the beginning of his story as an enchanter.

James's thoughts came rushing like an army for battle about his mother's power stone, defeating Burton for good, and stopping the threats and harm by witchcraft with their evil powers. James whispered to himself with his strong sense of courage and great determination.

"Peace will come!"

He closed his eyes after a long day awaiting to wake to a new sunrise. James's true capabilities as an enchanter are yet to be discovered, and a battle that seeks justice to the Pinnacle of Aries, and in James's life the battle just began. More than a battle, more than a story but a legend that saves an entire world of gifted powers that deserves peace and goodness.